the REBEL

New York Times & *USA Today* Bestselling Author
KENDALL
RYAN

About the Book

I never thought I'd see her again.

We shared one hot night together back in college before our paths took us in different directions.

But now, the most brilliant and beautiful woman I've ever met is back in my life. And the chemistry I remember? It's more combustible than ever.

Except...our fling is forbidden and must exist only in secret. Her rules, not mine.

I can't be her forever. I'm not that guy, and even she knows it.

But I can't stay away from her either. I'm determined to claim not just her body but her heart, even if that's the one thing she's vowed not to give me.

Playlist

"Pardon Me" by Incubus

"Bittersweet Symphony" by the Verve

"River of Deceit" by Mad Season

"Drive" by Incubus

"Wish You Were Here" by Incubus

"Blurry" by Puddle of Mudd

"Don't Look Back in Anger" by Oasis

"Shimmer" by Fuel

"Today" by the Smashing Pumpkins

"Hemorrhage" by Fuel

1

EDEN

"**D**on't look now," my best friend, Gretchen, says with a knowing smirk. "Here comes trouble."

Don't I know it?

Alex Braun is six feet of hockey god with a side of naughty trouble. Problem is, I like being a little naughty. When it comes to him, anyway. What good girl doesn't have a little streak of bad inside them?

But one stolen, *perfect* kiss aside, I'm still not sure Alex actually even knows who I am.

And who am I these days?

In high school, I was the governor's daughter. The first daughter of a wealthy, conservative family, I was smart and driven and unflinching in my beliefs.

Now, though? Three years in at Sutton, the small Boston university that has become my new home . . . I'm changing, and so is my family.

My dad is no longer governor. No, that ended horribly with a scandal involving his secretary, and my parents are no longer married. And me? Well, the itch to do something reckless is right there, clawing at me from just below the surface. I want to do something that's for me and me alone.

And Alex Braun is at the very top of that to-do list.

Gretchen knows this, which is why she's currently elbowing me in the ribs as Alex steps into the crowded living room.

Parties on frat row aren't usually our thing, but the hockey team won their game tonight, which meant they'd be out celebrating. Which meant the chances of running into Alex again were excellent. So I dressed in a pair of tight jeans and a cute black tank top, curled my hair, and dragged Gretchen out with me.

Alex lifts the cup to his mouth again, taking a long drink. One of his teammates practically mauls him, and Alex's perfect mouth breaks into a happy smile.

I'm transfixed by his chiseled jaw. Straight white teeth. Messy dark blond hair. Mischievous nature.

"Tonight's the night," Gretchen says, and I nod.

"Yeah," I mumble, momentarily struck inarticulate. The nerves swimming inside my belly are part excitement and part fear. The fear of rejection is strong, rearing its ugly head whenever I imagine going up to Alex and telling him what I want.

And what I want is *him*.

Our kiss last weekend at a party similar to this one has replayed through my head all week. Alex is responsible for a lot of crushes all over campus, but I felt something that night, a spark between us. For one brief, shining moment, his eyes met mine, and I was no longer the boring coed with straight As and too many responsibilities. I was someone fun and daring and desirable.

For him, it was nothing more than some stupid dare, but for me, it was much, much more. Goose bumps rose on my skin, and my heart pounded out an uneven rhythm.

Alex's mouth was shockingly erotic, hot and commanding, and my knees literally trembled. I reached out, pressing one hand into his firm shoulder for balance, needing the support if I had any hope of remaining upright. His tongue touched mine in confident, measured strokes, and I let out a little hum of satisfaction.

Which is really no surprise. Alex has a certain reputation on the hockey team. The guy can score. His room practically has a revolving door of gorgeous girls all looking for one thing—a hot night of fun. And I'm not ashamed to admit that I'm no different.

Over the past week, I've done some digging and learned that Alex is on a full athletic scholarship for hockey, that he's a top recruit, and is expected to be drafted into the NHL next year instead of finishing his senior year at Sutton.

Which means I need to make my move quickly, before he moves on.

Plus, I'm not the type of girl to sit around and wait for things to happen. I'm more of a grab-life-by-the-balls type. At least, I am lately. After my dad's fiasco, I learned that nothing lasts forever, and it's best to take what you can, when you can.

But my window of opportunity is shrinking right before my eyes.

Gretchen and I watch as a perky blond member of Kappa Nu approaches Alex. He smiles at her as she speaks, his gaze lowering from her lips to her ample breasts. Her mouth twists into a smile, and then she takes one of his big hands and tugs, leading him across the living room and up the stairs. And Alex follows like a puppy.

My stomach drops to my knees.

Gretchen meets my eyes with a worried look. "Shit."

I shrug, trying not to let her see my disappointment. "It's fine," I lie.

It's irrational, but the flare of rejection stings. Coupled with my family's fall from grace and the high expectations for me to succeed, it's too much.

I've imagined Alex and me as a power couple. Him the athletic sports star with the big smile and fun-loving attitude, and me with the brains and drive and connections. He'd see what a perfect match we'd make and abandon his fuck-boy ways. Every guy's gotta grow up sometime, right? And if Eden Wynn isn't the kind of girl you settle down with, then who the hell is?

My mantra is in my last name—Wynn at all costs. It's what I do.

Gretchen is still watching me with a worried look.

"I'll be right back. I'm going to find something

different to drink." My voice comes out steady, but inside, I feel anything but. I feel like I'm spinning out of control, like I'm on one of those tilt-a-whirl rides at the carnival.

Gretchen's expression darkens but she nods. I'm not quite sure she believes me, but I don't care.

Hurrying, I make it up the stairs in time to see Alex and the girl disappear into a bedroom. My heart hammers out a painful rhythm. This isn't how I wanted tonight to go.

The door doesn't close all the way like I expect it to, and my feet stop moving, stuck here in the center of the hallway. I don't dare move because I'm certain the creaky wooden floorboards will give me away. The music from downstairs is only a distant thumping sound up here, which means I can hear the faint rustling of clothes.

"Jesus," Alex grunts.

I hate myself for it a little, but I dare to take one cautious step closer, then another, until I can see through the crack in the door.

The sight isn't one I expected. I thought there would be a passionate display of groping each other, arms wrapped around bodies, and kisses so hot you could feel them deep down in your soul. That's the kind of kisses I've fantasized about sharing with him all week long.

Instead, Alex stands like a statue carved from stone, muscular and unmoving except for his chest, which hitches with quick, shallow breaths. His gaze is downcast, focused on the girl on her knees between his parted feet. Her hands work quickly at undoing his belt buckle. I hear the clank of metal, and my heart squeezes.

I can't see it from this vantage point, but it's obvious the second she gets his cock free. Because her head bobs, and he releases a strangled sound.

"*Fuck.*" He groans, squeezing his eyes closed and fisting her hair.

I force a breath into my lungs and stagger one step back.

"Spying?"

The deep rasp of a masculine voice in the hallway startles me and I whirl around, my heart in my throat.

"No."

The word leaves my mouth at the same moment I register who's joined me in the hallway. *Holt Rossi.*

If Alex is the golden jock, then Holt is the

brooding loner. He's imposing and powerful, and standing here before him, I feel a little unsteady. He's huge, with a broad chest. Wide shoulders. Chiseled jaw. And he looks ticked off.

"I was looking for something else to drink. The beer is awful." It's not a complete lie.

"The drinks are in the kitchen." He gives me a reproachful look, but after another beat, he nods toward the hall. "Come on."

For reasons unknown, I follow him. Maybe it's because he believes my lie. Maybe it's because I *really* don't want to see and hear my crush getting a blow job.

Holt and I had English composition together freshman year, and two classes together sophomore year. In one of them, we were assigned partners for a semester-long project. Then he declared his major—criminal justice—and our shared classes stopped. This year, I've only seen him a handful of times. His hair is longer and he looks like he forgot how to shave, but his eyes are still the same dark gray, expressive with a hidden depth I've never quite understood.

He unlocks a door, and I follow him inside. It takes me a minute to realize we're inside his bedroom. It's a small room in what appears to be a converted attic, with wood-paneled walls and a sloping ceiling that makes him duck as we enter.

"You live here?"

He nods. "Moved in last semester. Free rent."

"Why would Theta give you free rent?"

I know he's not in the fraternity. I'm pretty sure he's against what all fraternities stand for—fun, camaraderie, and brotherhood. Holt Rossi doesn't like relying on anyone but himself.

"Because I tutor the underclassmen, and I do all the grounds maintenance. Lawn care, snow removal, et cetera."

I nod. "Gotcha."

Holt grabs a silver flask from his dresser and holds it out to me.

I certainly don't want whatever mystery liquor is inside. I've never been a big drinker, but since I lied and told him I was up here searching for something to drink, I don't want to blow my cover.

I accept the flask and take a small sip. It's surprisingly smooth, but the burn of whiskey lingers on my tongue.

When I pass the flask back to him, Holt brings it to his mouth, placing his lips where mine were a second ago as he takes a long pull. The thought of it sends a small flash of something foreign racing through me, and I look away.

His bedroom is sparsely decorated with a twin-size bed on a metal frame, no headboard, and a single pillow. I sleep with at least six pillows. Excessive? Yes, but I like what I like.

His dresser is tall and narrow. One of the drawers sags like it's been pulled from its frame and never quite settled back in the same way again. A desk sits under the small round window, groaning under the weight of textbooks and an ancient laptop.

For the first time, I wonder about Holt, about his history, about what kind of things he likes to do, what type of girls he dates.

If I'm the well-bred society type that people assume me to be, then Holt Rossi is the opposite. From a working-class family and here on a merit scholarship, I've heard.

It's only natural that I should wonder about him. Right?

"You're not his type." Holt's deep voice pulls me from my thoughts again.

"Huh?"

"Braun."

I lift one shoulder, trying to look disinterested, but Holt's words slice straight through me, stealing the air from my lungs.

When he passes me the flask this time, I accept it eagerly, grateful for the distraction. I take a longer sip, letting the whiskey warm a path inside me.

"Why wouldn't I be his type?" I wipe my mouth with the back of my hand.

"Because." Holt shrugs, taking the flask back and draining it. "You're a good girl. You give off girlfriend vibes. And I'm pretty sure Braun is allergic to monogamy."

His words sting, but I have to admit that, somewhere deep inside, they make sense. If it's true that Alex will be entering the NHL draft next year, why would he want to be saddled with a college girlfriend?

Holt pulls out the chair that's tucked neatly into the space in front of the desk and offers it to me. I lower myself onto it while he takes a seat on the end of his bed.

Whereas Alex is athletically handsome in a rugged, hockey-player kind of way with his thick thighs, bulky forearms, and messy hair, Holt gives off a hot bad-boy vibe. He's tall, even bigger than Alex, and judging by the rough stubble on his jaw, his face hasn't seen a razor in weeks. But his eyes are kind, warm like melted honey. I've always liked his eyes.

"It doesn't matter," I say at last, realizing Holt's still watching me like a butterfly captured in a net. "It won't be happening. Not now." I look across the room to the door where, only a few paces away, Alex Braun is probably fucking some lucky/poor girl's throat.

Holt's tone softens. "He doesn't deserve it, you know that, right?"

I can't figure out how he's so perceptive. How he seems to know what I've been planning with Alex tonight. Not that I'd ever admit it to him.

"It?" *It* is a crass way to refer to someone's virginity, and my tone more than hints at my annoyance.

"Your *devotion*," Holt says to clarify, one dark eyebrow raised.

I straighten my shoulders. "Oh. Right."

Holt clears his throat and looks away. I'm not sure if he's embarrassed for me or simply giving me a moment. I release a slow exhale and try to collect myself. My hands are still shaking.

"You have any more of that?" I tip my chin toward the flask on his dresser.

Holt's mouth lifts in a crooked smirk, and I think it's probably the closest to an actual smile I've ever seen from him. He doesn't give off any warm and fuzzy vibes, but at the same time, I feel safe with him.

I recall sophomore year, after studying together in the library, he insisted on walking me back to my dorm when we realized it had gotten dark outside. He waited on the stoop, even though it was raining and he was without an umbrella, as I unlocked the door. He didn't move from that spot until I waved at him from my second-story window. Then he dropped his chin and shouldered his heavy backpack before he stalked away.

"Sure." He rises from the bed and opens the top dresser drawer, producing the bottle from which I assume the flask was filled.

When he hands it to me, I twist off the cap and take a sip. I can already feel myself growing warm and slightly tipsy.

"So, what's your story?" I ask.

"My story?"

I shrug. "Your major. Life plans . . . you know."

I already know his major, but I don't want to seem like a creeper. I also know he works part time as a bouncer at the off-campus bar called the Tavern, a regular weekend hotspot. He checks IDs at the door and breaks up fights when things occasionally get too rowdy.

Holt shifts his weight. "There's not much to tell. I grew up in a small town in New Jersey, a few hours outside of New York. And I got out as soon as I could."

"Family?"

He makes an annoyed sound. "I guess you could call them that. No one I'm close with."

I nod. Despite the image the Wynns like to give off, I know what it's like to come from a dysfunctional family. "My home life was tough too. Probably not like yours, but still . . . tough."

Holt doesn't shrug or laugh off my discomfort when I say this. I'm certain he knows I come from money, and that my dad was the governor, so he could laugh in my face if he was so inclined. He could pat me on the head and patronize me about my little privileged life . . . but he doesn't.

Instead, he meets my eyes with a look of understanding. Not sympathy, not pity, but some kind of common ground . On some level, we're sharing our secrets, and it's more than I've done with anyone in three years at this school. Even with Gretchen.

Holt's attention is yanked away by a scuffle in the hall and loud voices. I turn my head toward the door, listening, wondering if one of them is Alex's. Wondering if it's time to go. Then there's a dull thud of someone being shoved into the wall, and the sound of furniture scraping across the floor.

"Stay here," Holt says as he goes off to investigate, leaving me alone in his bedroom.

Loud footsteps thump down the stairs, and I cross the room. When I peek into the hall, it's quiet and empty. The voices are downstairs now, angry male shouts, though I can't make out what they're saying.

The door to the room Alex was in opens, and I quickly shut Holt's door, tucking myself inside once again. The girl he was with says something and he laughs, then there are two sets of footsteps as they descend the stairs together.

I pull out my phone and see a text from Gretchen. Where are you???

Upstairs, I reply with shaking hands.

I have no idea why I still feel nervous and on edge. Maybe it's because I was almost caught for a second time tonight, only this time by Alex?

But I know that's not it. It's because I've been basically hiding up here with Holt.

A reply comes from Gretchen. There's a fight outside. I'm leaving. You okay or do you need a ride?

Alex and his flavor of the night are gone. So, why am I still hiding out in Holt's bedroom?

Making up my mind, I text a response. I'll be okay.

Suit yourself, Gretchen types back. Let me know if you change your mind and I'll come get you.

I text her back the thumbs-up emoji.

Holt still hasn't returned, so I pocket my cell phone and cross the room to his little wooden desk that sits under the window. There's a notebook on top, and when I flip it open, I scan the page, trying to understand what I'm reading.

I'D HAD ENOUGH OF THE MINDLESS GAMES
THEN YOU APPEARED
WITH EYES SO BLUE AND HAIR SO SOFT
I'LL NEVER BE THE SAME

Song lyrics? Poetry? I'm not sure, but I don't want to snoop. The sound of approaching footsteps pulls me away from the desk and whatever private thoughts are hidden away in Holt's journal.

Holt bursts into the room, breathing hard. He's holding his fist near his side, and his normally stoic expression is twisted into a scowl.

"Fucking frat boys," he mutters under his breath as I cross the room to him.

"What happened?"

He doesn't answer. Instead, he swallows hard, looking pissed off.

"You're bleeding," I say, appraising him with concern.

His knuckles are scraped, and there's a drop of blood at the corner of his lower lip.

"I'm fine, Eden. You should probably go." Holt's tone is flat, and he won't meet my eyes.

"I'm not leaving you like this."

I reach out to touch his lip. I have no idea why I do it . . . I've never touched Holt before. Maybe it's because I've never noticed his mouth before. His lips are full and soft, and I don't like the sight of blood marring it.

When he speaks again, his voice is softer. "Believe me, I'm fine."

I wave him toward the bed. "You're not fine. Sit down."

2

HOLT

When I first met Eden Wynn, I never imagined she'd become a bright spot in my otherwise dark, miserable life. But here she is, choosing to spend her evening with me, locked away in my bedroom, bandaging my swollen knuckles so tenderly that it feels like the air has been sucked out of my chest.

Her disappointment about losing Alex Braun is nothing like the pain I feel—the deep, all-encompassing pain that edges out all the happiness in your life.

But that's a story for another time, because Eden is perched beside me on the mattress. The scent of her shampoo is driving me fucking crazy, just like it always did whenever we worked together at the library. After we turned in our final project last year, I doubted I'd see her again. Not on a campus as big as this one.

But I did.

First, a few months ago—a fleeting glimpse of her walking across the quad, her bright, sunny smile warming me, even from a distance. And then again last month at the bar where I work, checking IDs on the weekend. She came in with her friend, the same girl she was with tonight downstairs. I kept a close eye on her that night, as best I could, to make sure she didn't get into any trouble. But Eden is a smart girl. She knows better than to accept a drink from a stranger, or to follow some drunk douchebag home from the bar.

"Who did this?" Eden says, snapping me back to the present.

When I meet her eyes, their icy blue color nearly knocks the breath from my lungs. Her brow is creased in concern. Or frustration. I'm not sure which.

Is her frustration directed at me, at my life choices—that I always find a way to get in the middle of shit? Or is she frustrated at the situation I've found myself in?

"Doesn't matter," I grumble. "I'm fine, Eden."

She huffs. "You're not *fine*. You were in a dang fistfight."

I chuckle under my breath, wondering if she ever curses, or if *dang* is the extent of it.

"What?" she says sharply.

I shrug. "Nothing. Just never seen someone so worked up over some busted knuckles."

She gives me a pointed look, pressing those full, kissable lips together. "And a swollen lip, by the looks of it."

"Doesn't hurt. I swear."

Shaking her head at me, Eden stands. She dumps the wrappers from the Band-Aids into the little trash can beside my desk.

A couple of the partygoers got a little too rowdy downstairs, and I helped them off the premises. A few punches were thrown out on the front lawn, but we're lucky it wasn't worse. Lucky that the cops weren't called. At least, I don't think they were. The last thing I need is to follow in my family's footsteps and end up in the backseat of a police cruiser.

I take another sip of whiskey straight from the bottle she and I were sharing earlier and try not to wince, because *shit*, it stings my split lip. *Bet that'll look cute in the morning.* But what I told Eden is the truth. It doesn't really hurt. I've had much worse, and I'll live. I always do.

She surprises me by sitting on the bed next to me again. I offer her the bottle of liquor, but she shakes her head. I'm sure she's about to leave, about to get up and walk out of my life for good, but instead, something else happens.

Eden shifts closer and raises her chin, tilting her face toward mine. When she meets my eyes, my heart begins to hammer hard. Her eyes are such a pretty shade of blue—deep like the ocean, and filled with such intelligence and curiosity.

"Why was Alex in there with her?" She nods toward the door, and then those blue eyes are back on mine.

My heart shifts into overdrive. "Because he's a fucking idiot. Because he takes the easy offering."

"Always?"

"Always," I say, my voice going soft again.

She smiles at me. "Thanks for . . . everything. For saving me from making a fool of myself. I guess it's just as well."

"I didn't *save* you from anything, Eden. Something tells me you don't need saving."

I don't miss the hint of a smile on her perfect mouth. But it's the truth. I know she can handle herself. She's brilliant, beautiful, and kind. A triple threat.

Eden relaxes back onto the pillows, seemingly content to stick around a while.

Meanwhile, I'm trying hard to figure out what alternate universe I've found myself living in, but then again, I don't want to think too hard about why she's here with me. Not when I could just shut off my self-doubts and enjoy it. And so I do.

As we fall into easy conversation, I decide I could listen to Eden talk for hours. I learn that she met Braun last week, that she's not sure about her major, that her roommate leaves coffee mugs out on the counter for so long they grow mold, and it annoys Eden to no end.

I chuckle at this, and she shoots me a look of disdain.

I shrug. "If that's the extent of your problems . . ."

She frowns at me. "It's not."

Somehow, I believe her. Something tells me her life isn't as bright and shiny as she wants everyone to believe.

We've been sitting on my bed for the last two hours doing nothing but talking. I've never had this much fun with a girl . . . completely sober now, having a deep conversation. It's kind of crazy, if you think about it.

We've covered a lot of topics. Talked about everything from our families to our favorite movies, the best and worst pizza toppings, and even what we want out of life.

Eden's goals are much loftier than mine. Mostly, I don't want to end up in prison like my older brother, or in rehab like my mom. Big of me, I know. Which is why it's insane that she's lying here with me, using my shoulder as a pillow as we stare up at the ceiling.

It's late, and I should probably help her get a safe ride home . . . but I don't want to. And considering I'm feeling greedy tonight, I have no plans to end whatever this is.

"Do you ever just want to say *fuck it*," she says, "and do the exact opposite of what people expect of you?"

I chuckle into my fist.

"What?" She props herself on her elbow and gazes down at me.

God, I love just looking at her.

"I basically had that exact same thought. Lying here with you . . . on my bed. No one would have expected this—Holt Rossi and Eden Wynn. But fuck it. Fuck them."

Wild horses couldn't drag me away.

"So you're saying this is unexpected . . . me and you." She says it cautiously, still looking down at me.

"Very. But in a good way." I give her a small smile, and for once it doesn't feel forced.

Slowly, I reach out and cup her cheek in my palm. She has the softest skin I've ever felt. Either that, or I've never noticed details like that with other girls. But Eden isn't just another girl.

Proving my point, she lowers her face toward mine. It's a slow, cautious movement. Nothing about her is rushed. She's graceful, elegant, and so fucking *potent*, I could burst.

Her full lips part, and when her eyes sink closed, I slide my hand into the back of her hair. My fingertips press softly into the skin at the base of her neck as I draw her down to me. And then finally, her mouth touches mine, her lips slightly parted. They're damp and warm, and she presses closer.

It's the best first kiss I've ever had. And the impact of it vibrates through my entire body.

First, there's the shock of how good and soft and warm her mouth feels. And then there's the rush of arousal that pulses through me from my chest to my groin in wave after hot wave.

She kisses me back eagerly, her tongue making greedy, slow passes against mine. The pleasure of her mouth eclipses any pain I'd felt in my lip.

By the time we pull apart, I'm breathless. And when those blue eyes open, staring deep into mine, it's like another kick to the chest.

The moment is quiet and intense, filled with such promise.

I open my mouth to say something—I have no idea what—but Eden only kisses me again, this time crawling on top of me to straddle my hips.

Fuck. Heat races down my spine, and my cock hardens instantly.

One hand still buried in her hair, I bring the other to the soft curve of her ass. A tiny gasp pushes past her lips. When her eyes open and find mine, her gaze is hazy with desire. Something deep and powerful passes between us without the need for words.

It's like every emotion I've ever felt flashes between us, and I see the recognition in her eyes. She feels it too, an anthem that only we know the words to.

Accept me.

Don't reject me.

Love me.

When I dive back in for another kiss, Eden moans again. It's the best sound in the world.

Squeezing her ass—which is thankfully more than a handful—*fuck yeah*—I draw her closer so she can feel the effect her body has on mine.

One slow kiss becomes two and then three. When my tongue touches hers, Eden reciprocates, deepening the kiss and making me groan.

I thread my fingers through her silky hair and kiss her pretty, pouty mouth like my life depends on it. While we kiss, she makes small, need-filled sounds that make my cock ache.

We can't do this.

Can we?

"Holt," she murmurs.

Her shy smile almost takes my breath away. She places one hand on my cheek and leans in for another kiss, giving her hips an experimental roll.

Fuck. She's torturing me.

Fun fact: If I don't get inside her in the next ten seconds, I'll explode.

I settle my hands on her ass and tug her even closer. "You're killing me. You know that?" My voice is husky, little more than a deep rasp.

"Me?" Her tone is wary, like she's not quite sure she believes me.

That's crazy, though. She has to know how stunning she is. Pretty. Soft. Petite. Kind. The list goes on and on.

The only thing I'm not clear on is why she's here in my bed, doing this with *me*.

Eden surprises me yet again, pushing her hands under my T-shirt and touching my stomach muscles. They're not from hours spent at the gym, or on the ice like her hockey-playing crush. My body was built on hard work and summers spent doing physical labor. But I doubt Eden's thinking about such things right now as her mouth moves to the stubble on my throat.

When I reciprocate and put my hands under her

tank top, Eden raises her arms, letting me pull it off over her head. She's bare beneath, and I waste no time filling my hands with her gorgeous tits.

I shouldn't be here. Shouldn't be letting myself do this. But for some reason, it's *my* hands Eden wants on her body tonight, and I'm much too weak to stop myself.

"Holt . . ." She groans my name again when my fingers find her nipples and tease.

Her back arches, and my mouth moves from her neck to her chest, where I suck and kiss her perfect breasts.

We continue to kiss for a long time. I alternate between her plush lips and her tits, which I can't seem to get enough of. But then Eden ups the ante yet again, unbuckling my belt and pushing her hand beneath my jeans. I groan as she strokes me over the fabric of my boxers. Her touch is careful and soft, but feels so good.

I lift her off of me, changing our positions so I can get her out of her jeans. When I unbutton them and pull them down over her hips, Eden shimmies, helping me. Soon, she's naked in my bed, looking like the most delicious treat ever. I kiss a path down her stomach to her hip bone. She jolts like she's ticklish, and I smile up at her.

When I put my mouth between her legs, she jolts again, but this time it's from the shock of pleasure, not nerves. She stammers out my name, pushing one hand into my hair, holding me in place right where she wants me. Not that I plan on going anywhere. Not until she's come on my tongue.

I suck and nibble and flick my tongue against her clit until she's crying out in gasping sobs of pleasure. Another sixty seconds and Eden comes apart, quaking against my mouth as I hold her hips firmly in place, kissing her sensitive flesh until her moans subside.

A hot shiver of satisfaction rushes through me.

Once I kiss my way up her body, Eden tugs me close, and this time when she touches me, she's brave enough to push her hand beneath the elastic of my boxer briefs. The touch of her delicate hand exploring me makes me dizzy.

"Is this okay?" she asks.

"Yeah," I say on a shaky exhale.

Eden brings her mouth to mine again, her tongue teasing my lips apart.

I shove my boxers and jeans down and the rest of the way off, then I break our kiss only long enough to haul my T-shirt off over my head.

Eden's hand continues its slow exploration, her fingertips trailing along my shaft, her hand reaching lower to cup my balls. It feels incredible, but she seems a little unsure of herself.

"Could you come like this?" she whispers, lightly stroking me.

"Grip me . . . harder," I manage to say. "Yeah, like that." I put my hand around hers, showing her how to touch me. "Now drag your hand up."

She does, and the breath shudders out of me.

"Like that?"

I find her mouth again and kiss her hungrily while trying not to make deep, inarticulate sounds of pleasure. I'm pretty sure I fail miserably.

Fuck, that feels good.

"God, I want you." *I've always wanted you.*

"Then have me," she whispers back.

The prettiest three words I've ever heard. But she can't mean that.

Her hand stills against me. "Do you have a condom?"

The words hang in the air between us.

"I . . ." Long awkward pause. *Breathe, dude.* "Why?"

Smooth, Holt.

"So we can be safe?" she says, her lips lifting in a smile.

"I'm not fucking you, Eden."

My entire body throbs with the displeasure of that sentence leaving my lips. But it's the right call. It's the only call if I don't want to hate myself in the morning.

"Why not?"

Why not? Because she'd end up regretting it, and I don't think I could handle knowing Eden regretted sharing my bed. Tonight is already way more than I ever expected to share with her.

Don't ruin it, Rossi.

"Because it's not what you really want."

"Don't tell me what I want." Her eyebrows knit together in frustration, but I smooth them with my thumb.

"You want revenge."

She weighs my words, considering them carefully as she narrows her eyes again. "That might have been true before . . ."

"But not now?" I touch a lock of silky blond hair that hangs over her shoulder. It's even softer than I imagined it would be.

"Not now."

I bring my hand between her legs again and rub her clit. She's wet for me, but I'm not sure if we should go further.

Eden moans, and her hips move against my hand.

I reach under my bed for the box of condoms I stashed there earlier this semester but have never used. When I remove one from the box, Eden tears the package open and then hands it to me with an expectant look in her eyes.

I put it on, and then she climbs on top of me.

Holy shit. Are we really going to do this?

I can't help the slow grind of my hips. She's wet and pressed right up against me, the heat of her pussy driving me crazy, even through the condom.

"Wait. Stop." Her voice is breathless.

"Have you done this before?" I ask, my hands shaking.

Those gorgeous blue eyes meet mine, and she shakes her head. "Does it matter?"

"It matters to me."

"No, I haven't," she says in a soft voice.

"Fuck, Eden. Then we shouldn't."

She lifts on one elbow. "Don't you want to?"

A dark chuckle pushes past my lips. "Of course I want to. Look at you." My calloused fingertips skim her milky soft thigh. She's beautiful. Perfection.

Much too perfect for someone like me. Damaged. Broken.

I change our positions again so that I'm on top. Eden looks like a goddess with her golden hair spread out on my pillow and her blue eyes blinking up at me.

She parts her knees and I touch her calf, bracing myself above her with my cock in my hand. I rub the tip of it along her damp center, and she makes a pleasure-filled sound that hits me square in the chest.

"We shouldn't," I say weakly. *But fuck, do I want to.*

"Just do it."

With a slow inhale, I steady myself above her and push in about an inch—just the wide tip—into the tightest heat I've ever felt. Pleasure ripples through me, and I draw in a slow, shaky breath.

My hips flex, inching forward again, but at the same moment, Eden winces in pain. I look down to see her eyes are squeezed closed and her fingers are gripping my forearm. Immediately, I stop and then withdraw.

She looks up at me in confusion. "I said go ahead."

But I'm already pulling off the condom and tossing it into the wastebasket across the room. "Not tonight. I don't want to hurt you."

She gives me a soft, almost grateful look, and I know I made the right call.

"There's no hurry," I say, but I can barely hear my own words over of the rush of blood thrumming through my veins.

"We can do other things," she says.

A chuckle pushes past my lips. "I like other things."

With two hands on my chest, Eden gives me a little shove. I lie down on my back and then she's lowering herself until she's eye level with my groin. She gives my dick a quick appraisal and then meets my eyes.

With a smirk, I lace my fingers behind my head, and Eden laughs.

"I've only done this once before," she says, lifting my cock from its resting place on my stomach and treating it to a soft kiss. "Is this okay?"

A war of emotions clash inside me. First, yes, this is so much more than okay. And second, the desire to hunt down the dude she did this with—and tear him limb from limb—flashes through me.

"It feels good," I say instead, touching her cheek with my thumb. "Can you grip me tighter. Move your hand . . ."

"Like this?"

"*Fuck.*"

She smiles and licks my cock while her hand continues stroking.

It's not long before I feel the familiar tingle at the base of my spine. Her mouth is hot and looks so pretty moving along my dick. It's too much.

"Eden, fuck. I'm gonna . . ."

Her lips close around me as I erupt. The orgasm rips through me with such force that I jerk into her mouth. It seems to go on forever until I'm breathless and light-headed.

When I look at where she's perched between my knees, she's smiling sweetly at me.

"Good?" she asks.

"*Fuck,*" I mutter again. "Get up here."

I haul her up the bed until she's sprawled out on my chest. I want to get her off again, but Eden seems content to lie here with me. When I look down at her face, her eyes are closed. She looks sleepy and relaxed, and I smile.

It takes me a while to relax because I still can't believe she's in my bed.

Eden Wynn is in my bed. Never in all my years did I ever think this was a possibility.

Eventually, I fall asleep with Eden resting on my chest and my arm around her waist, holding her close.

• • •

In the morning, the only reminders that Eden was here are her lingering scent on my pillow, my almost empty bottle of whiskey, and the torn notebook page she's left on my desk.

My heart rate increases as I anticipate what she could have written. Did last night mean as much to her as it did to me?

But as I begin to read, my lungs expel a sharp breath.

THIS WAS A MISTAKE.
I'M SORRY. I HAVE TO GO.

Her words are hastily scrawled.

But their effect on my heart, unfortunately, is much longer lasting.

3

EDEN

Six years later

Holt was right that night. Alex wasn't worthy of the gift I saved for him, but I gave it to him anyway. Several months later, which is a story for another time.

Alex and I dated for almost five years, and I supported him through everything. His grueling training schedule, the wins, the losses, the cross-country trades. I even moved to freaking Canada for him, which ended disastrously one season later when Alex got in a fistfight with his own goalie and was released from the team.

Alex was the reason I became interested in hockey. My grandfather owned the team in Boston for as long as I could remember, but I never cared about hockey until I started dating Alex. Then I went to every game, proudly wearing his jersey as I cheered from the box, and cried when his team won their conference finals. My grandfather loved my newfound interest in the sport he'd spent much of his life working to further. Finally, something we could share.

But then my grandfather passed away, of pneumonia of all things. He spent six weeks in the hospital, the last three hooked up to a ventilator before quietly passing in his sleep.

And now I'm the first female owner of a major hockey team, and the youngest owner by more than a dozen years.

My critics laugh at me behind my back. Sports commentators make somber predictions about how long I'll last. No one has any faith in me. I'm not even sure I have faith in myself.

Fun fact . . . After I was named team owner, protesters gathered outside the arena. People made signs—signs with my name on them—demanding I sell the team because they think I'm going to run the franchise into the ground.

Yeah, I might fail spectacularly, but I'm going to do everything in my power to keep that from happening.

For the last several years, I've lived and

breathed hockey, and shadowed my grandfather's every move for the past three. Once he saw how serious I was about the franchise, he took me under his wing. I think we both assumed I'd spend ten or more years under his guidance, preparing for a leadership role in this organization.

But I only got two.

Because while Grandpa Pete was healthy, he'd also smoked for forty years. It did irreparable damage to his lungs, and he wasn't strong enough to fight off the pneumonia-like illness he came down with last winter.

Even when they admitted him to the hospital, our family wasn't concerned. "He's as strong as an ox, Eden," my dad said, smiling. "He'll pull through."

I believed that. We all did. Even when Grandpa Pete was sent to the ICU and hooked up to a ventilator. After he was sedated, I could no longer speak to him, could no longer ask him all the burning questions I still needed answers to.

Three weeks later, he was gone. It still doesn't quite seem real. And now I'm the owner of a struggling hockey team.

I feel lost. Alone. And scared.

These are new feelings for me. I've always been so confident, ready to tackle anything that comes my way. And of course, I can't admit to anyone how absolutely terrified I am. *Never let 'em see you sweat*, my grandfather used to say. I have to make him proud . . . except there's one more issue I have to contend with. And it's the elephant in the room no one dares to talk to me about.

Alex Braun has been traded to my team in the off-season.

It was his dream to play for Boston, and now he does. I can't help but wonder if that's why he dated me to begin with, because of the connections I have.

Was our entire relationship some big ruse?

Well, too bad for him, because although he might have gotten his dream job—a spot on one of the country's most-loved hockey teams—he now works for *me*.

The Boston Titans acquired him as a new trade in the off-season *before* I was named my grandfather's successor. Alex Braun is now our starting center, and I'm the brand-new owner.

Our breakup six months ago has been spectacularly splashed across the sports media outlets, dominating the headlines. It was annoying. And accurate. Because while I once loved Alex Braun, I can't stand the bastard. Things ended abruptly, and with a lot of animosity between us. Cheating rumors swirled in the media and on gossip blogs.

I don't know what to believe, but I know I'll never go back to being Alex Braun's girlfriend. On top of that, the season is set to start next week, and I don't know how I'll survive the shit show that is about to become my life.

Good times.

"Morning, Miss Wynn."

Lester Benson peers at me over a mug of coffee. He manages the front office and is invaluable to me, both personally and professionally.

Too absorbed in this expense report I'm going over, I didn't hear him come in.

Les pauses beside my desk, leveling me with a heavy stare. He was Grandpa's right hand, working together with him for almost two decades. I trust the guy completely, and am so thankful he's taken me under his wing.

He's almost like a father figure, which is nice, given that my own father can't figure out why I'm interested in this sport at all. Dad wanted to sell the team off to the highest bidder after Grandpa's funeral. I had to fight for it. And Les helped me.

When I look up and meet Les's eyes, he looks tired, like he hasn't been sleeping well.

"We need to talk about your security detail."

"Not this again." I roll my eyes. "I don't need a babysitter, Les."

Oh, that's the other thing. Apparently, I've been getting threats. Nothing credible, as far as I know, just a couple of angry fans most likely looking to stir up trouble. Some people don't like the idea of a woman in charge, especially a young woman with perky breasts and no wrinkles.

But I know hockey, and I love this team and won't let us fail. I'll make my grandfather proud. And I'm certainly not about to let one dickhead of an ex-boyfriend, or a couple of cranky fans, stop me.

Les sets his mug on my desk and gives me that fatherly look that always melts my heart. "With the season opening days away and your schedule jam-packed . . . traveling and staying in hotel rooms, living alone when you're here . . . it's the smart move, Eden. You know it's what Pete would want."

I swallow. Grandpa Pete would have been adamant about my safety . . . Les is right about that.

There would have been no room for negotiation on this topic if he were still alive, and yet that's all I've been doing for two weeks. I don't want to give in, but I'm tired of arguing.

The team already has a security crew. All they're pushing for is to add a security contractor to look after me.

"Fine. If you must. But he'd better know to stay out of my way and let me do my job."

"Of course, Miss Wynn." Les's bushy gray eyebrows lift. He was close with my grandpa, and I know Les misses his presence in these offices almost as much as I do. "It's already been arranged. Your new head of security will be here in fifteen minutes so you two can get acquainted and set up some parameters."

I heave out a long exhale. "Fine."

Pressing my fingers against my temples to stave off an impending headache, I blink at my laptop screen. It's been so hard to focus since Grandpa died. It's like all my motivation up and vanished. I can't concentrate on one task for longer than ten freaking minutes, and it's driving me insane.

Somehow I doubt that that's going to get any easier with some bodyguard watching my every move. I value my personal space and my independence, and I'm not in the mood to play nice right now. There's too much to do. Too much riding on this.

The intercom on my desk phone buzzes, and my assistant's voice rasps pleasantly through the speaker. "Miss Wynn, I have a Mr. Rossi here to see you."

Rossi.

My eyes widen, and I glance at Les.

"Oh, good. He's early." Les nods, oblivious to my sudden panic. "He's the best there is, just like Pete would have wanted for you."

"Thanks, Aspen." Swallowing, I straighten my knee-length pencil skirt as I rise from my desk. My high-heeled feet carry me toward the door on unsteady legs.

Les follows, and we both pause as my fingers curl around the doorknob.

"Les, what's my new bodyguard's first name?"

"Not a bodyguard. Think of him as extra security. You're an extension of the team now."

I roll my eyes. "Fine. What's my new head of security's first name?"

"Holt, ma'am. Holt Rossi."

4

HOLT

Eden made her choice all those years ago. She left my bed, with a hastily scrawled note as her only good-bye, and it was Alex she ultimately chose.

Even then, I couldn't bring myself to regret that night we shared. I knew I was on borrowed time with a girl like her. There's no way a guy like me, an imposter, would wind up with her in the end. The real world doesn't work that way. I was nothing more than the blue-collar guy providing a cameo in her too-rich-for-my-blood world.

But for one blissful night, she was mine. She bandaged me up and laid her head on my chest, the scent of her floral shampoo filling my head and affecting my judgment.

On paper, we don't make sense. Her family is

practically royalty, her father the former governor of Massachusetts. Old money, with a mansion in the city and a vacation cottage in Chappaquiddick. Yeah, they've had their fair share of scandals, but that's how it is with the wealthy. Sometimes they get caught, and other times their transgressions get swept quietly under the rug. That's just the way it is.

My family? It's a stretch to even call them that. We share DNA and nothing else.

I have an older brother doing time for armed robbery, a father who split when I was little, and a mom who's been in and out of rehab so many times, I've lost count. We didn't have big family gatherings or a turkey on the table at Thanksgiving when I was growing up, and there weren't wrapped presents under the tree for me when I was little. By the time I hit my teens, all I wanted in the world was my shot to get *out*.

In high school, I applied for every scholarship I could find. When the letter from Sutton University came offering me a full ride, for a second, I almost threw it in the trash. It was too good to be true. My older brother was probably fucking with me, sending it as a joke.

Except it wasn't a joke. The letter was real, printed on Sutton's letterhead. I ran my thumb across that raised emblem so many times, I wore it down to practically nothing.

The email address for the lady in admissions was real too. She replied two days later with all the details about my financial aid package.

Going to Sutton got me out, just like I'd always wanted. But the girls I met there, girls like Eden? Well, I knew they'd never want a guy like me, not once they learned the truth. And I told Eden so much of my truth that night.

Looking back, I have no idea why I even did it. Normally, I'm so guarded with my history. The less people know, the better. But those big blue eyes locked onto mine, and all this shit started spilling out like word vomit. I couldn't lie to her. And having the chance to keep that pretty blue gaze directed my way for a while . . . it felt damn good.

But just as I predicted, by morning, the spell was broken and Eden was gone. Never to return to my bed.

I have to say, though, I didn't expect her to be the one to tame Braun. The guy was a douche and a player, but it seemed, at least for a time, that he set aside his playboy ways and became devoted only to her.

Seeing them together was a punch to the gut.

Catching glimpses of them on campus was one thing, but seeing them together on the news sites was another.

Eden only grew more beautiful with age, and my resentment for Alex Braun deepened with each passing year. They were the media's golden couple, constantly photographed together at hockey games and charity events. Paparazzi hiding in palm trees even caught shots of them stealing relaxing moments at a tropical resort in the Caribbean.

Fucking annoying is what it was. Especially because the closest thing I've ever had to a tropical vacation was that time I took a wrong turn on the interstate and ended up on Long Island.

And now I'm here—at Elite Airlines Arena—about to come face-to-face with Eden Wynn again.

I don't follow the news coverage of her these days like I used to. But I know she and Braun broke up. That her grandfather died, and she's now the owner of the Boston Titans.

Her high-profile job means she's attracted some enemies, and it's going to be my job to protect her.

Time will tell if I can do that without losing a piece of myself again.

• • •

Six years is a long time. I should have been more prepared. But maybe you never fully get over the one who got away. Maybe there will always be some small part of me that wonders . . . what if?

And when I enter Eden's office, my first thought is not a very professional one.

Holy hell. I want to bite into her like a cookie.

My greedy eyes drink her in . . . from her long dark-blond hair that curls slightly at the ends, to her killer figure encased in a simple black pencil skirt and a silk top. Her eyes are as blue as I remember, but they seem deeper, wiser somehow.

I guess that makes sense. She's been through some shit since I last saw her, losing her grandfather and enduring a very public breakup. Things like that can take a toll on a person.

"Miss Wynn." I tip my chin in her direction, keeping my expression cool.

A smile lifts her full mouth. "Really, Holt? I think we're beyond last names at this point, don't you?"

I return her easy smile, pretending I'm not basically losing my shit right now. "I don't know. It's been a minute."

"A minute . . . or five years?"

"Six," I say, correcting her. *Shit*. I sound like I'm keeping score, and I guess I am.

Eden's smile widens a little more at my admission. "You're right. But at any rate, call me Eden."

"Of course," I say, and then my next thought manages to slip out. "It's good to see you again."

She motions me over to the empty chair at the conference table in front of the floor-to-ceiling glass windows in her office. There's no handshake or friendly hug, and I'm grateful for that. Because while I'm holding it together, I don't know how I'd manage touching her.

The older guy seated at the table in her office has been watching our interaction with an amused expression. "You two know each other?" he asks when I sit down.

Eden lowers herself into the chair across from me. "We go back a ways. Since college."

"Sutton?" the guy asks.

"That's the place." I nod. "Holt Rossi. It's nice to meet you."

He grins in my direction. "Les. Good to meet

you too. I was worried you were going to have your hands full with Eden. She didn't want extra security brought in, but . . . seems like with you two being old friends, maybe this will work out after all."

Eden chuckles. "Never discount my ability to be a pain in the ass, Les. I'm sure Holt will have his hands full with me soon enough."

A man can hope.

I clear my throat. "Should we begin? You can fill me in on the current security staff roles and responsibilities. Any gaps or shortcomings you've noticed?"

Eden straightens her spine and places her elbows on the table. She's all business now, and the playful side of her I glimpsed when I walked in is gone.

I'll be honest, though. This side of her is every bit as hot.

Be professional, I remind myself. I'm here to do a job.

"We employ the usual security staff of a professional hockey team," Eden says. "We have a director of security who oversees the department, which includes seven full-time security personnel, a couple dozen public safety officers who work the parking lots and perimeter on game days, and event security who enforce the rules for ice access, making sure no one approaches the players or locker rooms. Then we have technical staff who monitor our security systems and cameras. Everything is top of the line."

She pauses, smiling as she meets my eyes. "I've learned a lot these past couple of months."

Since her grandfather died, I assume she means. She's had to jump in with both feet.

"Sounds like you've got a handle on it. But now you're looking for some extra help? A contract position to keep Miss Wynn . . . *Eden* safe?"

Man, it feels weird having her name in my mouth after all these years.

Les nods. "Some extra help, yes. She's young. Single. And she's become somewhat of a controversial figure."

"Any credible threats?" I ask, my stomach tightening. "Emails? Phone calls?"

"No, nothing like that." Les shakes his head. "A few angry fans, comments on blog posts, things like that."

"Keyboard warriors," Eden says flatly.

Les clears his throat, directing his attention back to me. "This is all just a precaution. It's what Pete would have wanted."

I look to Eden. "My condolences about your grandfather. Of course he'd want you to be safe." After Eden gives me a sad smile, I continue. "I started my company four years ago. Before that, I worked in private security, learning the industry. We're small, only four employees right now plus myself, but I trust the guys I have completely. We'd be at your beck and call day or night."

I don't miss the way Eden's gaze lingers on my mouth as I speak. *Focus, Rossi.*

Les fills me in on the boycott of Eden when she was announced as team owner, a couple of small protests that really don't sound like they amounted to much. But still, he's right to take precautions. You really can't be too careful.

I nod along. "It reminds me of the same thing that happened years ago when a ninety-year-old grandmother took over a professional football team. That didn't go over well either."

"The fans can be pretty protective of their team," Les says.

"Misogynistic is the word I think you're look-ing for, Les." Eden's lips lift into a smirk at him before she turns those baby blues on me again. "And you're prepared to take on another contract? I travel with the team sometimes."

I nod. "Yes. And my staff can provide backup if I can't be somewhere, or if we need to secure multiple locations. We're trained in everything from how to handle a medical emergency to disarming a threat, dealing with atmospheric conditions, and taking care of special needs for female clients."

"So you'd carry her tampons and warn her if there was a thunderstorm coming?" Les says with a chuckle.

Eden lifts her brows at me as she waits for my response.

"Um, no. I'm pretty sure Eden can carry her own hygiene products, and that she's more than capable of interpreting her weather app. It's more about protecting our female clients from unwanted male attention, sexual advances, or even assault. And when I say atmospheric conditions, what I mean is when a person is outside of their normal environment, it can create issues if the individual isn't accustomed to the altitude, humidity, even jet lag due to changing time zones. All of these factors can cause a person's critical thinking skills and physical performance to suffer, making them a more vulnerable target. We're trained to keep an eye on things like that."

Les nods thoughtfully. "I see."

Most people have no idea what security guards do. It's a lot more than just watching for bad guys and talking into walkie-talkies.

Although the walkie-talkies are pretty cool.

"Sounds like a plan to me, son. We could use the peace of mind that our fearless leader here is safe." Les stands up and extends his hand toward me. "I have to get going. My wife has me trying this new thing—couples yoga. Says I need to open up more. Find my inner balance." He rolls his eyes.

I return his handshake. "Enjoy, sir."

And then Les is gone, leaving Eden and me alone together in her office.

I try to keep my gaze on hers. I certainly can't let it stray to check out her tits like I want to. It's surreal to be sitting across from her after all these years.

Unable to take the silence, I pull a business card from my pocket. "If at any time you feel unsafe, this is my personal cell number."

She takes the card and sets it on the table in front of her, frowning as she stares down at it for a moment. "Les is right. Everything you've said sounds good."

"But?"

She looks up and smiles. "But I don't know . . . isn't this going to be weird? Shouldn't we talk about things?"

"Things?" I raise an eyebrow.

"Our past," she says to clarify, tucking her long hair behind one ear.

My heart rate jumps. "It's really not much of a past. It was a one-time . . ."

I can't help my mind from flashing back to that night in my room. The way she kissed me, the soft moans of pleasure she made when my mouth latched onto her—

Eden holds up a hand, jolting me out of my memory. "I know. And I just left. You probably wondered what happened, why I . . ."

Fuck yeah, I wondered. I've done nothing but wonder for six long years.

But I shrug, trying to act as casual as she seems to be about this whole thing. "I get it. I was a temporary stop, princess. What's done is done. You don't have to try to make me feel better about it."

She flinches at my use of the word *princess*.

Shit. I don't mean to be an asshole. I guess it just comes naturally for me.

Sitting up straighter, she says, "But I—"

I lean back, feigning a casual posture as I interrupt her. "It's in the past. Let's move on."

"Okay," she says softly. "I can do that if you can."

"I'm a professional."

Her lips tilt up in a smile again, and her gaze roams briefly across the expanse of my shoulders, and the athletic black knit polo I'm wearing with my company's logo over my left pec. "I can see that."

5

EDEN

I wasn't much more than knee high when Grandpa Pete bought the Boston Titans. One of my earliest memories is walking into the arena hand in hand with him the day he signed the papers.

From that day forward, hockey and the Wynn family have been intertwined, and Elite Airlines Arena has become like a second home to me. A different company had the naming rights back then, back when the Boston Titans were claiming regular championship titles. There were more than a few legendary games in those years, or so I'm told.

As I got older, I was always much more interested in the catering options than the score. That and the fact that having access to the owner's box of a nationally acclaimed hockey team made me popular with the boys at my prep school, regardless of whether I watched the games or not.

But all that changed when I started dating Alex. When the man you love is at risk of getting his teeth knocked in, you learn to keep your eyes on the ice. Falling in love with the game was merely a lucky side effect.

I came to crave the smell of the arena, that musky mix of icy air and sweat, and even the hollow feeling of a loss was better than not watching a game at all. I guess I'll always have Alex to thank for that, although I'd rather not give him credit for any part of my life. Not since he walked out of it in favor of sowing his wild oats.

Now, less than six short months after he broke my heart, I'm watching Alex Braun play once again, but not from the stands like I used to. Now I have a view from the ice, and my eyes are locked on him for a whole new reason. I may have lost my girlfriend title, but I've swapped it out for a new one. *Boss*. A drastic upgrade, if I do say so myself.

"Two on one, boys. Do it again!" Coach Wilder's gruff, commanding voice barks from beside me.

I watch as the players glide to their marks, running through the mechanics of the drill. But it's just that. Mechanical. Unnatural, even. Like they're six separate units going through the motions instead of one cohesive team.

When Reeves, our left wing, weaves down the ice, Alex shoulders into him at full speed, which earns him a shove up against the boards. I wince at the hollow thud, turning toward Coach Wilder, who looks rightfully frustrated, if not a little pissed off. Something tells me this isn't the first time this has happened today.

My eyes narrow as I watch.

Bax, one of our best right wingers, rushes down the ice and comes up fast behind Alex, who struggles to maintain possession of the puck. It's sloppy, not at all like Alex to be so unsteady on his skates. He skids to a jarring stop in front of the crease without completing the pass.

Sweat plasters Alex's hair to his forehead under the helmet, and his chest rises and falls with quick breaths. His smile is usually crooked and lazy, and most times, easy. But today it's nowhere to be seen. He doesn't look particularly pleased to be appraised by his ex-turned-boss.

But that's exactly what this is, an appraisal, and I don't miss a thing. The way his gloved hands shake, the uncertainty in his eyes as he scans the ice.

I know Alex possibly better than anyone, and right now I know he's *not* very happy. The last several years floated by with Alex by my side. After college, we became one, me working part time and taking graduate-level courses in whatever city he was playing for at the time, and Alex playing his heart out to become one of the best young forwards in the league. Salt Lake City, Toronto for a season, New York for another. We strolled along the city streets, window shopping and daydreaming together about our future. We ate our meals at the little dining table I moved with us from city to city, and we made love regularly and enthusiastically.

We were young, happy—and in his case, very talented with a hockey stick—and nothing could stop us. On the nights he was home, I cooked while Alex sat on a stool in the kitchen, watching his game-day videos and critiquing his performance. I always encouraged him, and he would listen to me talk about whatever my latest pet project was.

When we lived in Toronto, it was volunteering once a week at a women's shelter. In New York, I became interested in running and joined a running club, though we moved away before I had the chance to compete with my group in the half marathon we'd been training for. The off-season was spent near family, or vacationing someplace warm.

Summer gave way to fall, and winter rolled in. Our months together turned into years as Alex and I built a life together.

What we had worked. At least . . . until it didn't.

I'd like to tell you there was a *moment*, a distinct time or event that made everything fall to pieces. But it wasn't as simple as that. While Alex traveled with the team in New York, I began spending time with my grandpa in Boston, learning the business of running a sports franchise. That was when Alex and I started to drift apart.

Things were changing. He'd still sit with me while I cooked, but he seemed more withdrawn. He didn't ask me questions about my day anymore, and when I wanted to tell him all the things I was learning from Grandpa Pete, Alex seemed far away and distant. Our sex life, which had always been regular and fulfilling, became infrequent and less satisfying.

Late at night, I'd try to talk to Alex, ask if there was something bothering him, but he'd only turn his back to me in bed, saying that he was tired. I worried he was cheating on me—it had to be the only explanation for this new distance growing between us, but I could find no evidence of that. Still, I worried because I often heard rumors about professional athletes having a different girl in every city, and I was terrified of losing him.

We fought sometimes. I accused Alex of being with someone else, and he accused me of being insecure. But I was desperate to know if he had someone on the side, and what she was like, because I wanted to be like *her*. Wanted to feel like I was still enough for him, even though I knew I no longer was.

Finally, when I couldn't take Alex's chilly indifference toward me any longer, I confronted him. He'd just returned from a three-day road trip to the Midwest. I'd cooked his favorite dinner—steak and garlic bread.

We sat calmly at the dining table, talking about his win over Cleveland, but inside I was so nervous, I was shaking. I was terrified we'd reached the end of our relationship, and I wanted desperately to hit rewind and go all the way back to the beginning when I was sure Alex loved me.

I started off carefully, tiptoeing around the subject of where we now stood. We felt more like roommates than lovers, and while I'd once been certain we were heading toward an engagement and marriage, now those things seemed oceans away.

Looking nervous, Alex dropped his head into

his hands. His refusal to meet my eyes made my stomach drop.

"Is there someone else?" I asked, blood pounding in my ears.

"No," he croaked.

It was of little consolation, because even if it were true, I could feel the years of love between us crumbling as surely as a child's sandcastle in the waves.

"Talk to me," I begged, tears welling in my eyes.

He stood from the table and paced back and forth. "I just need some space, Eden."

Space? From me?

The word seemed foreign to me. I loved Alex more than anything in the world and wanted to spend all my free time with him by my side. We had more than enough *space* when he traveled for games. Too much, really. I missed him terribly on the nights he was away.

But I could do nothing but sit there and listen as Alex paced and told me about his feelings of missing out—of being tied down so young and not getting to sow his wild oats. Talk of his teammates not inviting him out to a bachelor party because they thought of him as one half of an old married couple.

His words were like daggers shoved into my chest. My heart ached, and I was breathless. I latched onto words like *young* and *single* and something about us being *too serious*.

I remembered the reputation he had as a ladies' man back in college, the kind of guy who didn't want to be tied down. Why hadn't I listened back then? Been more careful not to give him my whole heart?

Sobbing, I asked, "Did you ever love me?"

Calm as ever, Alex met my eyes. "I'm sorry." And then he wheeled his still-packed carry-on out the front door and left.

I dumped our dinner dishes into the sink, poured myself a glass of vodka, and drank it straight. It tasted awful and burned my throat, but I welcomed the bitter sting.

Wasn't that what I deserved? To feel awful? I'd been so foolish, and now I felt broken.

I curled up on the couch and cried for two days.

• • •

My thoughts are interrupted by shouting on the ice.

It's Alex and Price St. James, a guy normally known for making his teammates laugh. He's not laughing today, though. Scowling, he throws his stick on the ice in disgust.

Well, that just happened.

I take a breath. Now is not the time to reminisce about my breakup, not that I want to relive the painful memories of the weeks that followed, anyway.

"All right, that's enough for today. Hit the showers, boys," Wilder calls out, pulling off his kelly-green Titans cap and shoving one hand through his sweaty brown hair. When he turns toward me, the look in his eyes is one of pure desperation.

"Well, that was brutal," he says with a rough sigh. "They're clunky as hell."

I've sat in on enough team meetings with the coaches to have developed a decent relationship with them, Wilder especially. Like me, he got his fair share of flak a year ago when he signed on as the youngest coach the team has had in decades. And while I hate to base our professional relationship on the fact that we've both been harassed by Boston sports fans, I have to count my allies where I can.

"They're blowing it," he mutters, looking out onto the ice. "We've got a lot of talent, but it's being wasted right now."

I nod, watching as the players disappear down the chute toward the dressing room and out of earshot of this conversation. "Any particular guys giving you trouble?"

"Nah, it's the whole team," he grumbles. "I know you don't want to hear it, but they're not on board with you as owner."

My lips pull into a tight frown as I step back, folding my arms over my chest. "I see."

I try to pretend I'm unaffected, but *shit*, the truth stings. I figured my own team wouldn't be like those asshole reporters who question my every move. I love this team, but I guess it doesn't go both ways.

"It's not just you, though," Coach says. "It's Braun too. They haven't rallied around him as part of the team yet. And, well . . ." He sweeps his hand through the air, gesturing toward the ice and slowly shaking his head. "You saw for yourself how that's going. He's unstoppable, though. If they can find a way to click with him, with his grit, Braun could take this team all the way. He's distracted. On edge right now. But I know he'll be good again, once the team's on board, probably. The hockey blogs aren't wrong about that."

My stomach turns inside out at the mention of the blogosphere.

It's true, Alex Braun has been the talk of every sports podcast and fan site since we signed him a few weeks back. I can't scroll through my Twitter feed without seeing Boston's latest and greatest starting center, the six-foot slap-shot god the city is pinning their hopes and dreams on. If I'm the villain, he's poised to become the hero.

As if it weren't enough to see my ex everywhere I look, I've also had to see my own face next to his. Despite our breakup, we're still a hot topic.

Everyone has an opinion, and every opinion is the same—if Braun is anything short of being the team's savior this year, my mere presence is entirely to blame.

But I doubt that will be an issue. If I learned one thing about Alex during the years we were together, it's that hockey will always be his first love. He's an athlete through and through, a competitor, and nothing will get between him and the game. Even our breakup, or a trade to a new team that hasn't quite accepted him yet.

Coach Wilder is right—Alex is unstoppable

and will power through, one way or another. I just hope for our team's sake that the bonding takes place sooner rather than later.

"Maybe they should hear from you." Coach shifts, looking at me now. When I open my mouth but don't respond, he tips his chin toward the dressing room. "They've got their reservations about you. But I think once they know you, once they know you're serious, they'll get their asses in gear."

I straighten, brushing a loose blond strand back into my low bun and smoothing down my suit jacket. When I was named as owner, I sent an email to the entire staff and team, introducing myself, letting them know I was ready for a great season.

But maybe he's right. Maybe I need to make a personal introduction. Show them I'm serious about this team, even if I didn't plan to give a speech today.

"I'm game if you think it'll help, Coach Wilder."

"Please. Call me Wild. Everyone else does."

"All right, Wild," I say. "Lead the way."

I follow him off the ice, racking my brain for the right words to motivate a failing hockey team.

My failing hockey team. If we're going to have half a chance at the playoffs this year, these men need to clean up their act. *Fast.*

We pad across the rubber floors to the locker room door, which Wild shoves open with both hands, hollering with a voice loud enough to make a tornado siren jealous.

"Pants up, men, we got a lady present. Team owner coming through."

I can't help but stiffen at the coach's word choice. While I appreciate him making sure the men are decent, I can't help but resent him calling me a lady first, and team owner second. But I tuck my bitterness away for another time. I have a pep talk to give.

As I pass through the door, the icy air gives way to a cocktail of sweat and men's deodorant. Our facilities are top of the line and maintained by an expert cleaning staff, but no amount of bleach can chase away the unique cologne of a professional hockey team after two and a half hours of on-ice drills. But it's a smell I'm used to. It comforts me in some small way.

I step carefully around the Titans logo on the floor, finding a spot close to the center amongst a line of half-dressed men. Half of them don't even bother looking my way. They're preoccupied with their gear, shoving helmets into cubbies and whipping practice uniforms into the laundry bin.

But they're not the ones who bother me. What gets me is the other half, the ones who are staring me down like I'm the grim reaper. And in some ways, I might be. Because if these men can't grow a pair and accept me as their new team owner, it's going to be a death sentence for our season.

"Gentlemen." I dip my head in a quick nod as I scan the line of players, trying to make eye contact with each and every one, if only for a second.

At the very end of the line, my gaze locks with a familiar set of ocean-colored eyes, their cutting gaze sending a shiver racing down my spine. Fresh from the shower, Alex Braun stands in front of me in nothing but a pair of athletic shorts that hang low on his trim waist, his fingers scratching absently at his bare chest.

I can't help but steal a glance, checking the space on his left pec, right above his heart. My stomach deflates. He still has it. The dark-shaded heart tattoo that he got for me, a surprise for my twenty-fifth birthday. My initials used to be tucked in the design somewhere, but I see that he's since gotten it filled in, the whole heart now as black as a hockey puck. He didn't even bother to leave any bare skin to hold another woman's name someday.

I can't help but wonder if that was on purpose. I may have held his heart for a few years, but he's not the kind of man to be held down. Not by me. Not by anyone. It took me a while to see that, but now it's as clear as day.

When I finally drag my gaze away from Alex, my focus moves to the next face in the locker room, one that's every bit as familiar, although much less expected. Holt is standing in the corner near the back exit, his thick arms folded over his chest as he surveys the locker room with serious gray eyes. When he meets my gaze, his unhappy look fades.

I didn't expect to see him here, and a jolt of electricity races through me. I was prepared to deal with one bit of romantic history today, not two, if you can even call what Holt and I had romance. It was a one-night mistake, and I'm undecided if that's better or worse than the five-year mistake I made with Alex.

Either way, seeing the two of them here together is unsettling—the man I chose . . . and the man I didn't.

But guys like Holt Rossi have heartache written all over them. Back in college, I thought Alex was the safe choice. The golden boy, a fun-loving jock everyone adored. I'd wanted a little bit of fun, to break out of my shell and experience all that college had to offer. A hot fling. Maybe something more. But I wasn't looking for *love*.

Against all odds, that's what Alex and I found together. He said I wasn't like the other girls he'd dated. Well, the term *dated* is a generous one. Back then Alex was known mostly for casual hookups. His few relationships had only lasted a couple of weeks—just long enough for him to get bored and move on to the next groupie. I guess I was the exception. I challenged him.

We worked well together. For a while, anyway. We weren't the best at communicating. Sharing with each other about our needs was never a strength, but then again, we were young. Each other's first loves. I'd like to think I've learned a thing or two about myself since then.

And now with some age and perspective, I question if Alex was the safe choice at all.

I know it's a waste of imagination, but my mind can't help but play out alternate versions of my past. Versions where I didn't run from Holt's bed and into Alex's arms. A version where I stayed with Holt and enjoyed his tenderness for a little longer.

If I had, would I have spent those years by

Holt's side? Would I still be there now?

But there was nothing easy about being with Holt that night. The way he kissed knocked me over—it was like drowning, gasping for air, but not wanting to surface. His mouth was so hot and insistent, I could barely breathe. It was too much, but not enough at the same time. Like water brought to a boil, flooding me with relief and a hint of danger. But my complicated and confusing emotions fell by the wayside as I gave in to what my body wanted.

And that night, I wanted *him*.

The way Holt looked at me, I can still remember it. Gazing deep into my eyes as if to memorize their color. His fingertips skimming my skin like I was the most precious thing in the world . . .

Snapping me out of the dangerous memory is Wild's low voice.

"Miss Wynn?"

Wild's rough chuckle brings me back to the moment, where I'm face-to-face with twenty expectant men, all waiting to hear what I have to say.

Heat rushes to my cheeks. *What has gotten into me?*

Here I am, dressed in my sharpest power suit,

holding the attention of a professional hockey team, all of whom are in my employ. I should feel like I have the room in the palm of my hand. Instead, I'm caught up in my own ancient history and the two men who helped me write it. It's unprofessional, which is not the way I want to portray myself. Ever.

My hands start to tremble, so I form them into fists and cross my arms over my chest, gulping down my nerves and hoping whatever comes out of my mouth is half as eloquent as what my grandfather would have said at a time like this.

You can do this, Eden.

"I know the team is hurting right now," I say, trying to steady my wavering voice. "No one worse than me. Pete, my grandpa, was my mentor and my friend. I know many of you can say the same. But we can't let losing him turn into a losing season. It's not what he would want, and I sure as hell know it's not what you all want either."

A few players nod in agreement while others seem to find the floor more interesting. I clear my throat, demanding their attention, and clear as day, a snicker cuts through the locker room. There's no doubt in my head who the source is.

My gaze briefly wanders toward him, confirming what I already suspected. A tight, smug smile is pulling at Alex Braun's lips, threatening to shrink my confidence to the size of the thin, icy shavings on the blades of his skates.

"I'll tell you what else my grandfather would have wanted," I say, my voice firmer now. "For you to treat me with the same respect that you treated him. We need to rise above the drama and move forward. It's the only way this works."

Briefly, I pause, weighing the wisdom of my next words. *Fuck it.*

"I'll be blunt. You guys looked like shit out there today. And I, for one, don't want our critics to be proven right this season. I'm going to work my ass off for this team. Are you?"

I scan the team, noting a couple of nods of agreement. *It's a start.*

"My door is always open, so if you have any suggestions, I'm all ears. Let's turn this around, and make not only my grandpa proud, but each other."

Having said my piece, I swivel on my heel, not allowing myself even a second to assess the team to see if anything I said stuck. Instead, I make a clean exit, letting my pumps carry me as fast as possible across the locker room floor. I don't even spare the extra steps to walk around the team logo this time.

So what if it's bad luck? No amount of bad luck could be worse than what I already have.

I rush toward the elevators, stabbing the call button as hard as I can. When the big silver doors part, I hurry inside, turning to jab the DOOR CLOSE button. But before the doors can obey, I spot a tall, broad figure heading in my direction at a slow jog.

"Hold the door," Holt calls, his voice low and rich, like caramel syrup being poured over chocolate ice cream.

For half a second, I weigh my options. I could pretend not to hear him. Let the elevator doors close and finally be alone, where I can fall apart without an audience.

But something in me reacts instinctively. Against my better judgment, I extend one hand, keeping the doors open long enough for Holt to step in next to me. When I pull away, the doors slide closed, and then it's only him and me, truly alone for the first time since I fled his room my junior year.

That was six years ago, and in that time, this man has only grown larger, in every sense. He was always bigger than the other guys during his Sutton days, but the man standing beside me now is pure muscle. His company-branded black polo hugs his thick biceps, the fabric stretched across his broad chest. When he speaks, his deep voice fills every inch of the small space we share.

"Are you okay?" he asks, his expression soft but serious.

I can't hold his gaze without facing the uneven heartbeat thrumming in my chest, so I turn my focus to the elevator buttons instead and lie. "I'm fine."

"You don't seem fine."

Damn him for being so perceptive. My shoulders sink as I deflate, the weight of the last ten minutes fully crashing down on me.

Of all the people in the world, Holt Rossi is the furthest thing from my chosen shoulder to cry on. But he's here, and he's ready to listen. One more look into those smoky gray eyes, and my fragile heart opens up.

"It's all just . . . a lot harder than I thought it would be," I whisper to the floor.

"What is? Having Braun here? Or taking your grandfather's place?"

I scoff, looking up to offer Holt a weak smile. "All of the above."

His eyes shift, deepening with a kindness I can't quite describe. "Understood. It's a tough job, I'm sure."

"Grandpa left some big shoes to fill," I say, swallowing the tears needling my throat as I wish with all my heart that Grandpa Pete were here now.

"And what about Braun?" Holt lifts one dark brow, his head tilting with curiosity.

"What about him?"

"Do you still love him?"

My heart leaps into my throat. *Did he really just ask me that?*

I study the tiny crack between the elevator doors, wishing I could shrink down to nothing and slip out through that tiny space. But there's no escape. It's only Holt and me, and the question no one else has had the courage to ask these past six months.

"No," I finally say, my voice soft but honest. "I'll always care for him in my own way, but it's not love. Not anymore. Not even close."

Holt nods, his full lips barely parting, like he's about to ask a follow-up question. But before he can say a word, the elevator settles at my floor, the doors easing open to allow for my escape.

"Well, this is me," I say as I step out, grateful for the abrupt ending to this mini press conference.

My heels click against the white marble tile as I hurry down the hall toward my office, not even pausing to look over my shoulder. I've done enough looking back for today, and all it's earned me is more hurt and confusion than I've bargained for.

6

HOLT

"So, you got it?" Madden asks, grabbing a pair of thirty-pound dumbbells from the weight rack.

"Huh?"

"The contract, dumbass. You got it?"

"Oh, right. Yeah." I smirk and help myself to a bottle of water from the mini fridge in the training facility.

Madden was the first employee I hired when I started my company. He's been with me for four years now, and we've grown from being mere boss and employee to friends.

Well, mostly workout partners, but occasionally drinking buddies too.

Today, though, our workout facility got an upgrade. Now that we're on the payroll of the Boston Titans, we have privileges at the same gym the players use. It's bougie as fuck, and I'm *not* complaining.

There are clean towels and free bottled water. Locker rooms that don't smell like fungus and sweaty balls. *Sign me the hell up.* There's even a juice bar in the entry with shots of turmeric (for inflammation) and ginger (for immunity, I think). I'm sure it's all a bunch of shit, but hey, it's the little things.

"Sweet, because after seeing this gym, it would be really hard to go back to using that shithole in your building's basement."

I chuckle. "Tell me about it."

Madden finishes his bicep curls and moves on to chest presses. "So . . . the lady boss, Eden Wynn. What's she like?"

I raise one eyebrow at him. "Lady boss? Really, dude?"

He shrugs and drops the thirties at his feet. "Sorry. Disrespectful?"

I lift my chin. "Not if you didn't mean it to be."

"I meant no disrespect. It's actually pretty cool

what she's doing. Making sure the team stays in the family, stepping up like that. Plus, a chick who likes hockey? That's just fucking cool."

I watch as he changes out the thirties for forty-fives. He must be working on his back next. "Yeah. She's cool. We've actually got a bit of history."

"Really?" His voice lifts on the question.

Shit. I shouldn't have said that. Of course Madden's going to want to know more.

"What do you mean by *history*?"

I pump out fifteen reps, taking my time. I would do more, put off having to answer his question, but my shoulders are screaming at me. They're still sore from my workout three days ago.

"We met in college. Freshman year, I think. Saw each other off and on after that. Had a couple of classes together."

"Shit. That's crazy. At Sutton, right?"

"Yup." I grab my water bottle and take another long drink.

"She's hot as hell."

I clench my teeth. *That's beside the point.* "We don't sleep with clients, Madd. You know that, right?"

My tone is patronizing, but I don't give a shit. Yes, Eden is gorgeous, but Madden is a known player. I may have to rethink scheduling him to work alongside her. I wonder if calling dibs would work. But Eden is a woman, not the last slice of cake at a birthday party. Or maybe I just won't take any days off for the next few months . . . that's always an option.

He grins at me and wiggles his eyebrows. *Fucker.* "Yeah, yeah. I know that. No sleeping with the clients."

As the boss, does this rule apply to me too?

It's a dangerous thought, but Eden's single. And I'm *very* single. *Shit*, painfully so. It's been a long-ass time since I've had any company other than my right hand.

But I can't think about that right now. Can't let myself wonder what it might be like to be with the grown-up version of Eden I met in her office. The suit-wearing, confident, badass *lady boss* calling the shots in a multimillion-dollar organization.

Down, boy.

When I look up, Madden is standing there staring at me.

"You don't have a thing for her, do you?"

I scoff. "No. I never had a *thing* for her."

Madden doesn't look convinced. After a long silence, he chuckles. "Shit, you *so* did. Probably still do. As I said, she's hot as fuck. And she likes hockey."

"Playing hockey isn't some great noble profession. You know that, right?"

He chuckles and shakes his head. "And security is?"

Shit, I need to stop talking. Next he's going to see through my disdain for hockey—the very sport Eden's ex-boyfriend plays for a living. *Smooth, dumbass*. And don't even get me started on the way Alex looked at her in the locker room today.

"Forget about it, Madd. I'm over it. Eden and I are ancient history. So, drop it, okay?"

"Whatever you say, boss." He grins at me again.

There's something about his playful grin that bothers me. Maybe it's because Eden seemed so rattled after her locker-room pep talk. I want to make things easier for her, not more difficult.

"I'm about done here. You?" Madden asks, re-racking his weights.

"Yup, but we're not skipping leg day next

week. Your calves are starting to look scrawny." I toss my damp towel at him.

Once we finish our workout, Madden heads out, opting to shower at home, while I plan to take advantage of the facilities here. It's probably better that he's gone. That way he won't see me order a ginger-and-turmeric shot, and then use it as ammo to make fun of me for the next decade.

This is a nice perk of working at the training facility. Even on my days off, I can come and use the gym here. A fancy-ass gym for the pro athletes. Never thought I'd be here, but I feel lucky to have landed the contract. Even some ribbing from my friend won't stop me from enjoying it.

Listening to Madden call me out about my crush on Eden was more than a little uncomfortable. It's scary how close he got to discovering the truth. But I'll protect our secret to the grave. As far as I know, Eden never told anyone about our night together, about her night slumming it with me.

I certainly never told a soul. But more than that, I got used to hiding that lost, vacant expression on my face whenever I spotted Eden and Braun together on campus. Got used to burying that hurt in my eyes, that look like someone kicked my puppy whenever they appeared together on the news.

That month they moved to Toronto fucking crushed me. It was the spring after she graduated from Sutton. There was a rumor that Braun wanted her to drop out the last few weeks of her senior year. If she had, I would have hunted him down and castrated the bastard. Anyone could see how important Eden's education was to her. When I heard she graduated with honors, I felt proud. Relieved. It was at least something she wouldn't compromise for *him*.

But then they left for Canada, and I thought that was it. Thought he'd propose, that they'd get married and live happily ever after. I was convinced I'd lost her forever. But I couldn't admit that to Madden. It was stupid. Young love. But that can't be right. An infatuation, maybe. It couldn't be *love*.

Then Braun fucked up in Canada. Fought with his own team's goalie during a game and was kicked off the team. He and Eden came back to the US, to Philadelphia briefly, then New York. Somehow Braun still managed to end up with a multimillion-dollar contract. That was a hard pill to swallow.

Although I had no right to, I mourned the loss of Eden, grieved like someone close to me had died. And my chances of ever being with a girl like her *did* die.

Through that experience, I came to realize what was possible for a guy like me and what wasn't. And being with a millionaire heiress to the Wynn fortune just wasn't going to happen. She'd made her choice, and I'd made my peace with it, but that didn't mean I wanted to fucking rehash it with Madden today.

Keeping memories of Eden in my past is easier said than done. As much as I try to pretend I wasn't affected, she still gets under my skin. The scent of her shampoo. The way she sucks on her bottom lip when she's deep in thought. Her bright-eyed determination. I love that she thinks she can run Boston's hockey empire with her sheer will.

And that's the thing about Eden. Of course she can, and she will. She'll prove all her critics wrong, and I guess I'll be the guy with a front-row seat to it all. What doesn't kill you makes you stronger. At least, that's what I hear.

I head toward the showers and select the one on the end. Thankfully, no one else is here today, so I have the place to myself. Cranking the water to hot, I push down my shorts and boxers and yank off my T-shirt.

Stepping into the spray of hot water, I let out a sigh. I grab my bodywash and lather up, washing my face, armpits, groin . . . all the important parts.

Now that I'm alone, my thoughts return to Eden. Watching her take charge of the guys, giving that speech. Hearing how composed and confident she sounded.

My hand drifts down to my dick, and I give it a slow caress. I'm already half-hard just from thinking about the way Eden looked in that suit, the way she commanded the attention of every guy in that room. She's a force to be reckoned with.

Forget it.

But it's not like I can ignore the rush of heat to my groin. I give the base of my cock a warning squeeze.

Now's not the time, dude.

Later, I promise myself.

If I keep this up, things with Eden are bound to get complicated. I shut the door on my past, but maybe I can open it just a crack. Just long enough to peek inside to see what I missed.

7

EDEN

"You're saving me one of those tortillas or I'm stabbing you."

My eyebrows dart up at the sight of our team captain pointing a plastic knife at one of the rookies. *Wow* . . . this is officially *nothing* like the elegant start-of-season banquets my grandfather used to host at his Victorian mansion in Cambridge.

I wanted to keep the well-loved tradition alive by throwing a small dinner party at my condo for all the players and their plus-ones. But this night is quickly turning into a mess. I ordered fajitas for forty-five people from one of my favorite local restaurants. We have twenty players on our roster. Add in the plus-ones that a few of the guys brought, and this should have been plenty of food.

I guess I underestimated how much a professional hockey team can eat . . . or how much room these big guys can take up. Luckily, the guys aren't shy about being practically on top of one another. Personal space is nonexistent in the hockey world, and after a few beers, no one thinks twice about three grown men piling onto a two-person loveseat.

As I wander through the kitchen collecting empty beer bottles, I'm warmed by the sound of comfortable chatter mixing with intermittent deep, rumbling laughs from the living room. For the first time since Grandpa Pete passed away, I feel welcome here among the team. As I should, I suppose, because this is my home, after all. But baby steps.

"Need another beer, Reeves?" I call out to our left wing forward, who's leaning against my granite kitchen island, gripping a long-necked bottle that looks close to empty.

He tips it toward me before draining what's left of it. "No, thanks, Miss Wynn. Too many of these, and I'll be about as useless at drills tomorrow as a donkey on skates."

I bite my tongue, holding back the very real truth that, based on what I saw on the ice the other day, a donkey on skates might prove to be an asset to the team. But Wild assured me that yesterday's scrimmage ran way smoother than the on-ice practices leading up to it, which is a much-needed sliver of reassurance.

"Well, if you change your mind, the fridge is stocked. And call me Eden," I remind him with a soft smile.

But while beer is in no short supply, I can't say as much for the food. After a quick sweep through the kitchen to stack the empty trays, I sneak off down the hall to place an emergency pizza order. If I'm going to avoid any accusations of trying to starve the team, we'll be needing some reinforcements.

Just as I press the COMPLETE ORDER button, my phone buzzes with an alert from the front desk, notifying me that I have more guests on their way up.

When I tug the door open, standing outside is Price St. James, one of the defensemen, who, like most of the players tonight, arrived with a six-pack of craft beer hanging in his grip. He hands it off to me, and I admire the colorful geometric design on the cans before thanking him with a polite smile. He's tall and broad-shouldered like all hockey players, but he's also got a quick smile and sparkling blue eyes. Everyone calls him Saint. I'm still getting used to the nickname thing. They all have one.

He steps inside, shaking his head at me when I go to close the door behind him. "Hang on now, my plus-one is just a few steps behind me."

I arch one curious brow, a smile tugging at the corner of my lips. "I didn't know you had a girl-friend, Saint."

Most of the guys on the team are single, a bit of information that the media loves to dwell on. Of all the players to be tied down, Price St. James seems like the least likely. When the tabloids aren't speculating which of the players I'll end up falling into bed with, they're posting pictures of Saint at the hottest Boston bars, surrounded by a new group of puck bunnies each weekend. And I guess those pictures aren't doctored, because my mere sugges-tion of his significant other makes him snicker into his fist, and a familiar chuckle agrees from down the hall.

My fingernails instinctually dig into the soft skin of my palms. I know that laugh all too well. It's Alex, the only member of the team I was hop-ing would pass on the invite to this dinner.

Anxiety builds in my throat. I should have known that the two biggest players on the team would buddy up, but just knowing that my ex has made a friend on the team leaves me feeling un-easy. It's a catch-22.

On one hand, I want everyone to think of Alex as poorly as I do. On the other hand, if they don't rally around their newest teammate, we're doomed for the season. Either way, my stomach starts churning the second he steps up to the door.

I instantly recognize the six-pack tucked beneath his arm. It's the same hoppy sour we used to keep our fridge stocked with. His favorite. Personally, just the smell always nauseated me. Of course that's what he chose to bring.

"The day Saint's got a girlfriend will be a cold day in hell," Alex says, shooting me a wink that gives me an instant wave of nerves.

Based on the way these two are laughing like old friends, I'd say the team is starting to accept Alex as one of their own. Now if I can just get them to do the same for me.

"Or maybe a hot day on the rink." Saint claps Alex on the back. "Whichever comes first."

"Hey, eez not so bad, Saint," Lucian Bisset, our goalie, hollers from the couch in his thick French accent. He has one muscular arm wrapped around his slender blond wife, who smiles as she sips daintily from a can of sparkling lemon water. "When you have a wife, zere eez always someone to be, how you call, Didi?"

Saint frowns, his dark brows scrunching together as he tries to interpret. "Didi? I thought your wife's name was Camille."

Lucian mimes turning an invisible steering wheel, then motions toward his half-empty beer resting on the glass coffee table. "You know. Tonight, she is my Didi."

Saint's blue eyes brighten with a flicker of recognition. "Oh, you mean DD. The designated driver." He doubles over with laughter, then crosses over to the couch to slap his hand against Lucian's. "Damn, I was gonna say, man. Whoever this Didi girl is, can I have her number? She sounds fuckin' hot."

"Language, Saint," Camille says, frowning.

"My bad, my bad." Saint laughs, lifting his hands in surrender. "What I meant to say is she sounds fuckin' *pretty*. Is that better?"

As the players laugh, Camille rolls her eyes, but she doesn't bother pushing the argument any further. It's not worth it, especially with Saint. Despite his nickname, everything about this man screams *sinner*.

"What about you, Wild? How's the single life treating you?" Saint asks, tilting his chin toward Coach.

Wild winces at the question, slowly shaking his head as he gulps what's left of his beer. From what I understand, he and his ex-wife finalized their divorce in the spring, right around the time Alex and I broke things off. There must have been something in the air.

"I'm not taking questions on the subject," he finally says gruffly. "Why don't you bug the rookie about it instead? He's the one who's been glued to the dating apps half the night."

Tate nearly leaps out of his own skin at that comment, shoving his phone into his back pocket before he can be caught in the act.

"Attaboy, rookie." Saint cackles, clapping Tate on the shoulder. "Get yourself some action."

Tate rolls his eyes, then his gaze bounces between Wild and me. "I—I'm just swiping," he mutters, his cheeks turning the slightest shade of pink. "I'll get off my phone, I promise."

"This isn't math class, Tate." Wild laughs. "Do what you want. Just don't come crying to me when you catch something that you need a prescription for."

"Camille, how are you and Lucian enjoying Boston?" I ask, hoping to steer the conversation back into safe territory. Because, *wow*. Seriously, do these guys have *no* boundaries?

Camille leans forward, placing her fingers on her chin. "Well, good. Is nice. But we're still learning American culture."

"Has there been anything that's surprised you?" I ask. I know that she and Lucian have lived in the US for about eighteen months now.

Camille considers my question. "The people here . . . Americans, you are very friendly. Very open," she says in her elegant accent. "Oh, and the portion size . . . It's way too much food."

This gets a chuckle out of a few of us, but Lucian only shakes his head. "Is fantastic."

"I have a new friend. We meet at dog park. She is dating and says the singles scene here is horrible."

A few heads nod around me.

No comment.

Camille continues, having captured an audience now. "She says American men are . . ." She waves one hand in a dismissive manner. "No matter, I am happy I have my mate."

"Just say it," Tate says.

"Well, she says American men . . . Why don't

you moan during sex?"

My cheeks begin to burn, probably turning a bright red. *Well, grab some popcorn because things are about to get salty.*

Camille's question pulls a deep chuckle out of Tate. "Um . . . I don't know. Years of silently masturbating so my parents wouldn't hear me?"

The guys laugh.

"That, and because I'm usually out of breath from doing all the work," Saint says.

Okay, so they're going there. I try not to squirm with embarrassment.

Reeves nods. "So many reasons. Trying not to come. Focusing on getting my partner there because I'll finish regardless . . ."

Camille leans forward in interest.

"I just yodel. I figure it's way sexier," Saint says with a wink.

The guys laugh, and someone slaps the back of Saint's head.

Alex doesn't contribute to the conversation, and I'm very grateful for that. The last thing I want to do is remember what he was like in bed. Though those last few months, we really had more of a roommates situation going on.

"I think it's bold of you to assume hockey players are having frequent sex," Wild says with a smirk.

This pulls a chuckle out of Alex, who has otherwise been a bit surly tonight.

As the conversation takes a crude turn, I duck back into the kitchen, rearranging the fridge to try to accommodate the six-pack Saint left on my counter. It's moments like these that make me wonder if hanging tight to my role as team owner was smart after all.

I'm sure that Grandpa Pete had no problem being one of the guys in situations like this, joining in on their conversations about women and dating. Although he'd been married for fifty happy years, he had plenty of wild stories from before he met Grandma, and the man was never one to miss a chance to tell a dirty joke.

Meanwhile, I'll never be able to chime in on a conversation like that without being accused of hitting on the players. And that's not a path I'm ever willing to go down again. Not just because it would be wildly unprofessional, but because I have almost five years' worth of proof that dating a hockey player isn't good for my mental health.

My phone buzzes with a notification from the front desk that the pizza has arrived, and I make my way back through the living room to the front door, pulling it open as I hear the first knock. But for the second time tonight, I'm caught off guard.

It's not the delivery man standing before me. At least, not the one I was expecting. It's Holt, carrying a stack of pizza boxes that obscures most of my view of him.

My body instantly reacts to his presence, tensing up at first, then flooding with a rush of warmth that takes me by surprise. My jaw hangs slack, and suddenly, words feel like a distant memory. There's only one word on my mind.

"Holt."

Not a sentence, not a greeting, just his name. It's all I can manage. I gulp down my nerves, pressing my shoulders back to summon any bit of confidence I can muster.

"I didn't think you'd come." *Smooth, Eden.* "I mean, thank you for getting the pizzas."

Holt shakes his head, although I can't see anything but his cool gray eyes from behind the stack of boxes. But just one look into those eyes has me feeling unsteady, the same way I did all those years ago.

"It was nothing. Delivery guy was in the lobby, asking the front desk about buzzing up to your unit. I volunteered to take it from there, save the guy a few minutes."

"Did you tip him?"

Holt's gaze narrows, and I don't have to see his mouth to know that he's smirking. "Of course I did. I'm not a monster."

I give him a warm smile. It's still so surreal having him here. "Well, thank you. Let me know what I owe you, okay?"

I take the stack of boxes from him, despite his protests that he's happy to carry them the rest of the way. It's a much-needed distraction to keep my mind from playing out all the ways I'd like to repay him. Maybe with another one of those toe-curling kisses we shared so many years ago. What was it about him that made me want to give him everything so quickly? I hardly knew him before that night, after all. But in the span of a few hours, this kind, mysterious man looked beyond my family status and saw who I truly am, a deeper part of me that I haven't shared with anyone since. Not with Alex, not with anyone.

And I saw Holt too. He invited me into the darkness of his past, the goals he had for after he graduated from Sutton. When we kissed, it felt like I'd known him all my life. I would have given him everything that night, had he not stopped us.

I bat away the memory with a few deep breaths, focusing instead on setting out the pizza boxes where the trays of fajitas used to be. Now is no time to be fantasizing about false realities. Not when Holt's own words are still echoing in my head.

"It's in the past. Let's move on."

I've barely opened the first pizza box when Tate appears with an empty plate, grabbing two slices and smashing them together like a sandwich.

Being that I didn't so much as taste a fajita earlier, I nab an extra-large slice for myself, draping it over a plate before escaping to the living room, which has quickly emptied, thanks to the alluring scent of pepperoni wafting in from the kitchen.

I settle into one of the leather loveseats, blotting the grease off my slice with a napkin before bringing it to my lips. The cheese stretches off the crust, like it should on a true East Coast slice, and for a moment, I feel at ease again. That is, until Holt takes the seat next to mine.

"Is this seat taken?" he asks, arching a brow.

"It is now. By you." There's an edge of sass to my voice that I wasn't quite planning on, but Holt doesn't seem the slightest bit bothered by it.

"Great. Because I thought you might need something to wash that down with."

I glance down to see a brown paper grocery bag in his grip. I didn't notice it when he arrived, what with the leaning tower of pizzas he was carrying, but now he has my full attention. The bag crinkles as he reaches in and pulls out a slender glass bottle filled with a light pink liquid. *Rosé.*

"It's your favorite, right?" he asks, presenting me with the bottle.

I accept it, careful to make sure our fingers only brush briefly on the handoff. But even that split second is enough for the electricity to leap from his fingertips to mine. "How did you know?"

"I may have asked your assistant," he says, a devious smile threatening the corner of his lips. "I actually thought about bringing it in a flask, for old time's sake."

A quiet chuckle escapes me at the memory of us sharing sips of whiskey in his room at the frat house. Now I feel a little sheepish about the fact I wasn't brave enough to extend the invitation for tonight's gathering to him personally. I had my assistant, Aspen, call him instead.

"I don't need anything to help me drink this stuff any faster than I already do," I say, grinning. "I'll grab us some glasses."

Before I can get up, Holt shakes his head, reaching back into the bag and pulling out an insulated cup that looks like a cross between a stemless wineglass and a travel coffee mug. "I got you this too. Figured you might need it with all the stress of your new job. You could bring it to the office. Maybe with coffee, though."

This time, my laugh is anything but quiet. "You have *no* idea."

And just like that, it's as if no time has passed between us. The six years that sped by between me scrawling a note on his dresser, and him stepping into my office last week, feel like the blink of an eye.

This is the same man I spilled my heart to after a few sips of whiskey, the one whose bloody knuckles I tended to, even when he insisted I could leave. The same man who, in a matter of hours, came to know me almost better than I knew myself. And that scared me.

But looking at him now, I wonder what it was that I was so afraid of.

8

HOLT

It's my first official day reporting for duty, and I have a meeting with Eden and Les at nine in her office at Elite Airlines Arena.

The first hockey game is only days away, and there's been some talk in the media about another protest. It pisses me off to think about what Eden has to endure. She comes into work every day to do her best, and yet some troublemaking idiots want to make her life more difficult. It only makes me want to help her more. Must be some underdog complex. Fuck the naysayers and all that.

The building is impressive—a steel-and-glass structure where the hockey team plays also houses the team leadership's offices. I've never been here for a game, but I'm sure the experience is quite different. The building is eerily silent and deserted on a Monday morning. A lone security guard waits at the main doors, and a cleaning crew buffs the concrete floors on the ground level, but other than that, it's quiet.

I make my way to the elevators, remembering the somber look on Eden's face the last time we were alone together here. She seemed relaxed enough at the team dinner at her place, so hopefully she's settling into her role here with a little more confidence.

When I reach the floor to her office, Eden's assistant is seated at a glass desk just outside her door. Her name plate reads ASPEN FORD.

"Hello." I pause in front of her.

She looks up at me and pulls a pencil from her mouth, then blinks at me twice. "Holt, right?"

"That's me."

Her mouth curls into a slow smile, and I wonder what Eden's told her about me. About us.

Probably nothing. Because there is no "us."

"Great. Eden and Les are inside. They're expecting you. Go on in."

I nod and then let myself inside Eden's office, pushing open the heavy frosted-glass door. They're already seated at the conference table, and Eden's gaze lifts to mine the second she spots me.

"Morning," I say.

Her full mouth lifts in a smile. "Good morning. You're right on time. Coffee?"

Today Eden's dressed in a pair of black pants, glittery ballet flats, and a pale pink blouse. It's decidedly feminine, and I love that she's confident enough to be herself. She doesn't try to mold herself to the standards of what others might say is needed for the leader of a sports franchise.

I shake my head. "Not a coffee guy. Thanks, though."

"Tea?" She pulls in a breath, drawing my gaze to the delicate gold necklace resting between her breasts.

My heart hammering, I force my eyes to meet hers. "I'm good, but thanks for the offer."

"I couldn't live without my morning joe," Les says.

Jeez. For a second, I forgot he was even here. It's easy to get wrapped up in Eden. She's striking and poised and so fucking tempting . . .

Stop, Holt.

Giving myself a mental shake, I take a seat in the same chair as last time so I have a view of both Eden and the door to her office.

"So, should we get down to business?" she asks, tapping her pen on the table beside a black leather planner embossed with her initials, EMW.

It occurs to me that I don't know her middle name. *Marie, maybe? Michelle? Mary?*

"The travel schedule is the first thing we should discuss," Les says, looking between Eden and me with a frown.

If he's worried I'm going to blow off traveling with the team, he's wrong. I take my role seriously. Even if that means flying to Saskatoon in the middle of January, I'll be there. I'll need to buy a new parka, but I'll be there.

"Whatever you need." I dig my smartphone from my pocket and pull up my calendar.

Eden smiles. "There's a home game this Thursday, and then we leave Friday midday for a game on Saturday in Detroit, and stick around the Midwest for a game in Ohio on Monday. We're back late Monday night. Probably not until midnight or so."

After jotting the dates and locations down in

my calendar, I nod to Eden. "Sounds fine. No issues here."

"I hope you don't have any pets." Eden's watching me from over the rim of her coffee mug.

Just like her outfit, her mug is unapologetic, sporting the phrase *Let's Keep the Dumbfuckery to a Minimum Today* written in fancy cursive writing. I have to squint to make out the words, and when I do, my mouth twitches.

"No pets," I say.

Her eyes lift to mine. "Not even a goldfish?"

For a second, I'm speechless, transported back in time.

It was something we talked about that night we spent together. Eden admitted that growing up as an only child, she was often lonely. She said she'd always wanted a pet, but her parents never allowed it. I stupidly suggested she get a goldfish. She teased me, saying fish were a big commitment, and she didn't know if she had the time.

"Haven't made the commitment yet. You?" I manage to say, my voice raspy.

With a laugh, she shakes her head, and Les watches us like we're insane.

Maybe we are.

"No pets," I say firmly. "No girlfriend. Just me."

Her gaze lingers on mine for a minute longer. "Still, I know it's a lot to drop everything and travel. So, thank you."

"You're more than welcome."

As Eden presses on with the fall's remaining trips and events, Les's cell phone begins vibrating on the table.

"Excuse me for just a minute," he says, standing and frowning down at the thing.

"Take your time," Eden says, enjoying another sip of her coffee as Les exits her office, closing the door behind him.

Now that we're alone, she turns her attention back to me. "Why aren't you dating anyone?"

The girl I once knew wasn't always so bold around me. I remember Eden as being sort of shy that night. Ducking her chin when I asked her a question, fidgeting and tucking her hair behind her ear. Ready to flee from my bed at any moment. That's the way I remember her.

But then something shifted. She let her walls

down and got comfortable. She opened up to me. We lay down together, and she rested her head on my chest. I liked that part. Never been much of a cuddling type of guy, but I enjoyed it that night with her. Hell, I enjoyed everything that night with Eden.

I realize she's still waiting for me to answer her question. The one about why I'm still single.

"No time, I guess. I probably work too much."

She shifts, still watching me from across the table. "I see. That makes sense. You've grown your company, your reputation. It's impressive what you've done."

I nod but dodge the compliment. "What about you? Has there been anyone since Braun?"

The second the words leave my mouth, I regret them. It's none of my damn business, but Eden doesn't seem offended or bothered by my question.

"No," she says softly. "Before he got sick, my grandfather tried to introduce me to his golfing partner's godson."

"Did you meet with him?"

She nods. "Yes, but it didn't work out."

"Why not?" I'm curious, and since she's entertaining my questions without so much as a pause, I'm rolling with it.

"There was no chemistry. *At all*," she says sternly. "He was about as exciting as a baked potato."

An easy chuckle tumbles from my lips. "Gotcha. So, we're both single."

A smile lifts her full mouth. "It would appear so."

Les comes back in, pocketing his phone. "How's it coming along, kids?"

"I think we're about done here," Eden says.

Les nods toward me. "You want me to show you around? I can give you a tour of the control room."

I stand. "Thanks, that sounds good."

I need to learn the facility where Eden works if I'm going to be here to support her, though my primary role will be shadowing her when she's away from this place—on the road, moving from city to city, hotel to hotel. But I have two hours to kill before I told my mom I'd visit, so I might as well make good use of it.

"Let me know if you need anything," I say to

Eden. "Otherwise, I'll see you on game day."

She nods, waving her fingers at us. "Have fun, boys."

We leave Eden behind, hunched over her laptop with that damn coffee mug.

Les and I use every bit of that two hours to get me acquainted with the building and the security systems currently in place. It's a state-of-the-art setup, and I'm feeling much more optimistic than I have any right to.

Because if life's taught me anything, it's that whatever can go wrong, will.

• • •

"You want something to eat?" Mom asks, opening her fridge and peering inside.

I don't know what she could be looking for, because she hasn't been here in six weeks. Surely whatever was in her fridge before she left for rehab is rotten by now.

Then again, maybe it's just a mom thing—asking your kid if he's eaten. And the truth is, I am hungry. I came right here from my meeting with Eden and Les and haven't had lunch yet, but it's not her responsibility to feed me. She can barely remember to feed herself, and the last thing I want to do is put pressure on her. My mom's always been a little bit . . . fragile. Unstable.

"I'm good. Thanks."

She nods and lets the fridge close. Stepping away from the kitchen, she runs her hand along the clean countertop, humming to herself. I sent a cleaning crew by a few days ago when I heard she was getting out, so she didn't have to come back to a dusty apartment.

"Everything go okay? You feeling good?" I ask, settling into the armchair in the corner of the living room.

"I feel just fine." She waves me off. "Between you and your brother, I swear, you're like two mother hens."

She chuckles to herself, but her humor is lost on me because, yeah, of course my brother and I worry about her. She's been addicted to pain pills for almost two decades. And I really hope getting clean this time will stick for her, but who the hell knows. I've learned to roll with the punches. One week she's doing great, and the next, I'll come by and find her as high as a kite.

"I just came by to make sure you were doing

okay. Getting settled in again." I say, carefully hedging.

She looks at me with irritation. "I said I'm fine."

"I know. And I wanted to tell you that I'm going to be gone for a couple of days, and more often coming up. I got a new job."

Turning in my direction, she smiles. "Yeah? Good for you, baby. Security for some big CEO or celebrity this time?"

I nod. "Something like that. You remember Eden Wynn?"

Her eyes flash with recognition. I made the mistake of mentioning once I had a history with the former governor's daughter.

Mom's expression hardens. "I thought you learned your lesson a long time ago. You'll never be enough for a girl like that."

With an annoyed breath, I rise to my feet. "It's just a job, Mom."

"Good. Because it won't do you any good to start thinking pretty thoughts about girls like her. I saw what happened last time."

She didn't know shit about what happened last

time. But then again, maybe she's more perceptive than I thought. Maybe she knew me withdrawing and closing myself off had a lot more to do with Eden's rejection than I let on.

"I know, Mom, don't worry. I've got to get going. Take care of yourself," I say as I hand her a few bills.

She curls her hand around the cash, giving me a grateful look. "I always do, don't I?"

I raise a brow in her direction. That's debatable. But the last thing I want to do is get into yet another argument with my mom. "Talk to you soon."

She only nods in response.

9

EDEN

It's strange to be working at my grandfather's desk, a dark mahogany piece of furniture, large and masculine. It suits the office nicely, but it doesn't suit *me*. I wonder how long I'll feel like an imposter.

Absently, I flip through a coffee-table book sitting on the edge of the desk. This one is filled with images of dramatic landscapes from around the world, photographed in black and white. I have no idea who bought it or why it's here. It's just a generic part of a generic office that I haven't made mine yet.

A photo near the middle of the book makes me pause—it's of a volcanic eruption. The sky looks normal, but everything around it has been blown to smithereens, the trees toppled over and bare of any branches or leaves.

I feel at home as I run my fingertip over the glossy image. Everything in my life looks normal. But inside, I feel confused and conflicted and distraught much of the time. Maybe everyone is right, and I need to sell the team and walk away with my dignity before it's too late. But some stubborn, selfish part of me won't let me do that.

Some days can only be conquered through pump-up playlists and double shots of espresso. The kind of days that begin with extra concealer under my eyes, and end with me falling into bed exhausted, with some whirlwind of chaos for the twelve to fourteen hours in between.

Lately, I call these days normal, and they're a gentle summer breeze compared to the tornado I've been living through the last week. Which is why, somewhere between observing the team's morning skate and my fifth brand-sponsorship meeting of the week, I sent an SOS text to Gretchen, insisting we pencil in some much-needed girl time.

Two hours later, she's booked us mani-pedi appointments at my favorite nail salon, and now, after making liberal use of the massage functions of this pedicure chair, I'm beginning to feel like a new woman.

As the cloudy water spirals down the drain of my foot bath, David, my favorite nail guy, slips a flimsy pink pair of foam flip-flops onto my freshly exfoliated feet, then motions me toward the manicure station. Gretchen has already settled in at her station for the fancy hot-towel treatment she booked, and I pad over to join her, tossing my long-empty coffee cup into the trash can on the way.

"You've got to stop drinking coffee this late in the day, girl," she says as I sink into the seat next to hers. She'd probably wag a finger at me too if her hands weren't wrapped in hot eucalyptus-scented towels. While I didn't spring for the deluxe treatment, just catching a whiff soothes my nerves.

"I will, I promise. Just as soon as the season ends, and I'm not losing half my sleep to stress dreams involving my late grandfather shooting hockey pucks at my head."

Before she can take a crack at psychoanalyzing that nightmare, David interrupts her, shaking a bottle of bold emerald polish in my direction. It's the perfect shade of Boston Titans green.

"This is your color, right?"

I nod, resting my wrists on the terrycloth towel. Normally I stick to pale pinks and nude tones, but if ever there was an occasion to paint my nails Titans colors, it's the first game of the season, which is in less than twenty-four hours. For my toes, however, I stuck to my favorite shade of ballet-slipper pink. Old habits die hard.

While David gets to work filing my nails into the perfect almond shape, Gretchen scoots her chair an inch or two closer to mine, turning her shoulders to lean into whatever gossip she's about to launch into.

"So, is it true that they're adding extra security detail for the team this year? I read this whole article about it, but some fans say it's just talk."

For David's sake, I try not to flinch. "Since when do you read the hockey blogs?"

"Since my best friend became the owner of a professional hockey team," she says, the *duh* implied. "And especially since said friend became the subject of some crazy protests."

My stomach clenches at the reminder. Things have quieted down a bit since the initial announcement, but I'm not optimistic enough to believe the fans are on board with me quite yet. "There's speculation of another march outside the arena before tomorrow's game too."

Gretchen frowns, worry brewing in her deep brown eyes. "Jesus, I'm so sorry. Who knew hockey fans could be such dicks?"

"And sexist," I say with a huff. "Sometimes I think this city would be happier with a golden retriever for an owner, so long as it's male."

"I, for one, think you're doing a way better job than a golden retriever," she says.

It's not much of a compliment, but it makes me laugh, which is something I haven't done a whole lot of lately.

"Well, I'm glad my fan club has at least one member. Maybe if we win tomorrow, I'll get a second and a third."

Gretchen's smile fades, her voice dipping to a strained whisper. "And what if you lose?"

I heave out a shaky exhale, focusing on the tiny nail brush David is wielding like a Michelangelo of manicures. Admittedly, I've been ignoring the very real possibility of a loss.

"Then maybe I'll be glad management hired the extra security. Personally, I think the protesters are all bark and no bite, but—"

"But you can never be too careful these days." Gretchen finishes my thought, then steers the conversation in a more positive direction. "I'll bet the extra security has you feeling better about things, though. Right?"

My heart kicks in my chest. I've been having plenty of feelings about our security detail lately, very few of them having to do with my safety. In fact, a hundred percent of those feelings revolve around a certain tall, smoky-eyed man who seems to be occupying the corners of my mind in the least professional of ways.

"Well, I'm feeling all kinds of ways. Actually, I've been meaning to ask you about one of our security guards. Any chance you remember Holt Rossi?"

She's silent, and my gaze wanders back to hers just in time to watch her nose crinkle in thought. "That name sounds familiar, but I'm drawing a blank."

"He graduated from Sutton the same year we did. Really big guy, kind of a loner type?" There's a whole arsenal of other more flattering adjectives I could use to describe him. Tall. Broad. Mysterious. A better kisser than any man has the right to be. Need I say more?

After another quick pause, Gretchen's eyes brighten with a flicker of recognition. "Oh yeah. Rossi. Wasn't he involved in breaking up that fight at the frat house the night you were trying to hook up with . . . he-who-must-not-be-named?"

"You can say Alex's name, Gretch," I say gently. "He's an ex, not a hex."

She shrugs. "I know. I just think he doesn't deserve to take up any more time in our conversations than he already has for the last six years." She gives me a sly smile.

I'll give her that. But I don't think Gretchen understands that working in close proximity to Alex is its own special kind of torture.

If only I didn't know how tense he got after a game, maybe my hands wouldn't itch to rub his shoulders. If I were able to forget how hard he was on himself following a loss, I wouldn't care about how hurt he probably was.

But caring for Alex is no longer my role. He made his decision. *He* was the one who broke things off, the one who wanted to be single, and he got his wish.

So, why doesn't he seem any more at peace? I'm not sure. But it's no longer my job to comfort him. Now he has puck bunnies for that. And according to some of the locker-room chatter I've overheard, he's making good use of *their* skills.

"Anyway, back to Holt," Gretchen says with

a wiggle of her eyebrows. "Did he remember you from Sutton or something?"

I nod, my teeth habitually finding my lower lip. I never told Gretchen about my one-night history with Holt. It didn't seem important enough to share at the time. It was just a one-time thing, after all. A fling. A fluke. So, when I slipped out of his bed and scrawled my good-byes on a scrap of paper, that was that. He was in my past, where I thought he'd stay.

And he did, up until now.

"Yeah, he, uh . . . he remembered me. And I remembered him too, of course." I can't disguise the nervous hesitation in my voice, and Gretchen catches it right away, her gaze narrowing with a devilish gleam.

"What's going on?" Her voice is a low, suspicious whisper. "Did something happen between you two?"

Something? Damn near everything happened between us, all in one whirlwind of a night.

I used to think Holt was a one-time thing. An error in judgment on my part. It used to bring me shame, thinking about my night with him. I went to that party determined to get the fun-loving hockey player to notice me, and instead hooked up with the rugged loner. Afterward, I felt ashamed, and Holt was the antihero in my story.

An adult now, I know better than to be ashamed of my actions that night. A hefty dose of hormones and misplaced lust sent me into Holt's bed. I couldn't blame myself. The man *is* very attractive, in a brooding, outcast kind of way.

"We actually, um . . . we hooked up once," I murmur, trying to keep this public conversation as private as possible.

Unfortunately, Gretchen doesn't take the hint on my preferred volume for this topic. Her jaw falls slack, releasing a sound somewhere between a gasp and a squeal. "Holy shit, no way. In the arena?"

"Oh my God, no," I whisper-shout. "This was back in college."

"Oh." She's quiet for a long moment, then her lips purse, suppressing a smile. "I kind of wish it was in the arena instead. At least I'd know you were getting some action since you-know-who."

"Sorry to disappoint," I say with a laugh.

"But wait, when in college was this? I can't believe I didn't know. Was this before we met?"

I shake my head. "It was actually the same

night you remember. The one of the fight at the frat house. I went off looking for Alex, and Holt found me along the way. And then . . ." A flush creeps across my cheeks. "And then we hid out in his room, drinking and talking, and . . ."

I don't finish the rest of that statement. David keeps his eyes down, focusing on my manicure. I'm sure he's heard much worse before, but still.

While David is gone to get the hot towels for my manicure, I dish to Gretchen on the details of that night, everything from the swigs of whiskey from his flask, to the hastily written note in the morning.

When I'm finished, I draw in a deep breath, the smell of acetone and apricot scrub serving as some small comfort as I wait for her reaction. But instead of one of the responses I'm expecting, like a *Wow* or *I can't believe I never knew that*, her brows shoot up to her hairline, urging me to go on.

"And then . . ." She presses for more, her eyes as wide as her smile.

"And then I started dating Alex a few months later," I say with a sigh. "And you know exactly how that story ended."

Disappointment flashes over Gretchen's face, then quickly fades to a small smile. "And then six years later, your hockey team just so happens to hire his private security firm."

"Yep. Crazy coincidence, right?"

"I don't think so." Her tone is matter-of-fact. "I think it's a sign."

A laugh bubbles out of me, but before I can tell her how ridiculous she's being, Gretchen's focus shifts to her manicurist, who keeps her gaze lowered and doubles down on buffing out the ridges of Gretchen's nails. By the time they're done discussing her desired nail shape, my best friend has other topics on her mind.

"So, what about you-know-who?"

My brows push together in genuine confusion. "*Do* I know who?"

Her eyes roll so far back, I'm momentarily concerned they'll be permanently stuck that way. "You know. *Alex.* Do you think you're over him?"

"Alex and I are done," I say firmly. "Plain and simple. If anything, he's helped me realize exactly what I don't want. No more hockey players, and no more cocky assholes."

"Huh." Her lips lift in a smirk. "So, someone like, I don't know . . . Holt Rossi?"

"Have you been huffing nail polish?" I tease. "What happened between Holt and me is so far in the past."

"College wasn't that long ago, Eden." She clucks her tongue, a self-satisfied smile spreading across her lips. "And do you really think it's just a happy accident that six months after your breakup, an old hookup from undergrad shows up in your life?"

"Yes, I do."

I'm being short with her now, but I can't let this turn into a legitimate topic of discussion. Especially not when Holt and I have already wandered into dangerous territory, discussing the fact that we're both very single at the moment.

Naturally, my brain ran rampant with that information. Hell, I even told him about my clunker of a date Grandpa Pete set me up on. Why did I do that? So Holt would know I'm open to dating? *Jesus.* Thank God Les didn't leave the two of us alone for too long. I could have let our chemistry carry us away.

"You're all set."

David caps the bottle of gold nail polish I didn't see him grab and dips his chin toward my nails, each one painted kelly green with a touch of sparkle added to the tips. It's the kind of perfect touch only someone who has been doing your nails every week for six months would know to do. The fluorescent lights bounce off the tiny gold flecks in a way that's almost hypnotic.

Maybe I can hypnotize myself. *You will not think about Holt Rossi that way. You will not think about Holt Rossi that way . . .*

Jesus, I really need to change the subject.

"So, you're coming with me to the game tomorrow, right?"

Gretchen's face sours, all her mischievous matchmaker energy disappearing in the blink of an eye. *Note to self—bring up sports anytime you need Gretchen to drop a topic.*

"Do I actually have to watch the game?" she asks with a whine.

"Come on, you're telling me you still don't care about hockey? Not even now that you're keeping up with the blogs?"

"I care about *you*," she says to clarify. "But I don't care about a bunch of sweaty guys fighting over a puck that, half the time, I can't even see."

"It's not their fault you need an updated contacts prescription," I remind her. "Maybe then you wouldn't have such a hard time keeping up."

"I told you, I'm *nearsighted*," she says stubbornly. "So as long as you keep the catering options *near* me, we won't have any problems."

A laugh spills out of me as I pull my credit card from my wallet. "Just don't get too close to Holt, okay? I don't need you talking to him about the fact that he's apparently a sign."

Gretchen holds up a freshly painted pinkie. "Promise to try my best."

I give her a pointed look. "That's not the same as promising not to talk to him."

She shrugs, then shoots me a wink. "I said what I said."

• • •

"Ladies and gentlemen, let's give it up for this year's Boston Titans!"

Looking over the stadium from the executive suite, I feel like a queen surveying her kingdom. The seats are packed to the rafters with fans, their raucous applause sending a jolt of adrenaline coursing through my veins.

It's been a stressful week, but tonight I feel nothing but pride. Every headache-inducing day and late night at the office has been leading up to this moment—the first game of the season. And I'm ready for my team to prove what they've got.

As the team shuffles down the chute and out onto the ice, the sea of jersey-clad spectators leap to their feet, fists pumping and cheers echoing through the stadium. Moments later, our competitors take the ice.

Let the games begin.

Beside me, Gretchen rests her elbows on the glass half wall, watching the teams warm up with a look of determination in her eyes. "Which ones are our guys again?"

"The green jerseys."

She frowns and squints. "But they're both green."

Stifling a laugh, I give her a reassuring pat on the shoulder. "The Denver Avalanche are teal, Gretch. Don't hurt yourself. You can go get food, if you want."

She brightens at the mention of hors d'oeuvres, almost enough to make her enthusiasm about the puck drop seem genuine. As soon as the forward for the Avalanche takes control of the puck, though, she scuttles off to the buffet, returning a few minutes later with a plate piled high with spring rolls and chicken wings.

"Want some?"

I shake my head. "No, thanks. I'm not very hungry."

The truth is, my stomach is probably about ready to eat itself, but my nerves have kept a vise grip on me all day, and I haven't been able to stomach a thing. Not unless you count the two oat-milk lattes I've sucked down to keep myself alert.

Maybe Gretchen has a point about my caffeine habits, but that's a conversation for another time. For now, my eyes are locked on the ice, my attention wandering only momentarily when I spot a certain broad-shouldered head of security standing one section beneath my box.

A fluttery feeling stirs in my belly.

Holt looks handsome as hell in that Boston Titans polo, even if the jewel tone does seem a little contrary to his personality. His usual black shirt and slacks complement his broody gray eyes and the dark stubble peppering his angular jaw, but I like him in green equally as much. Or maybe I just like the idea of him matching my nails.

That's a worrying thought.

I look away from him just in time to watch the Avalanche score the first goal of the game, and a few minutes later, the second. *Shit*.

All the things I used to know about Alex seem to be thrown out the window. He used to love the thrill of speeding down the ice, the rush of adrenaline with each hit, but right now he looks tired. Worn out. Completely over it.

It's strange because he should be at the top of his game. He's single, just like he wanted, and he recently signed a lucrative deal with Rush Sports, one of Canada's biggest sporting goods brands. And not that I went looking, but I see photos of him on the hockey blogs from time to time with different women on his arm. A blonde in a silver dress he took to the ESPN awards last month, and a buxom redhead he was photographed with leaving a nightclub the week after.

I'm proud to report that these sightings have no bearing on my emotional state. After our breakup, I cried all the ugly tears, ate all the ice cream, binged on so many vodka sodas, I didn't think I could ever enjoy one again. And now, it's as though Alex Braun has been purged from my system. I grieved the loss of our relationship, and my heart is in a good place—which is to say it's closed for business. The only thing I want to focus on at the moment is my career.

By the time I look back to where he stood, Holt has disappeared, replaced with a lankier blond guard who I don't recognize. I'm more than a little disappointed by the swap, but I didn't come here to stare at security. I've got a team to keep an eye on. And now we're down by two in the first period—which is *not* good.

"So, where's that steamy security guy?" Gretchen, who must be a mind reader, nudges me in the ribs.

She's no help in keeping my focus *off* of Holt and *on* my team, but I know my attention needs to stay on the ice right now. Only seven minutes into the first period, and the Denver Avalanche have already sunk two slap shots past Bisset. Not the start to the season I was hoping for, but we still have plenty of game left to turn it around.

"Hellooo?" Gretchen elbows me again. "Did you hear me? I asked where's that hot bodyguard of yours?"

"He's not my bodyguard," I say, correcting her as my eyes still chase the puck. "He's security for the whole team."

"But you're not denying I'm hot, huh?"

My stomach bottoms out to my kneecaps. That deep, husky voice definitely doesn't belong to my best friend.

I whirl around, and sure enough, there he is, his gray eyes burning into mine and sending a wave of heat pulsing through me. I don't know if I'm smitten or embarrassed, probably some combination of both, if I'm being fully honest with myself.

"H—hi, Holt," I stutter, nervously adjusting the tuck on my green cashmere sweater. Paired with the shade of beet red I'm sure I'm quickly turning, I'll bet I look like a freaking Christmas ornament right now.

Shit. Mental note to practice my poker face in whatever very limited free time I can scrounge up.

Finding my voice, I gesture to my best friend, desperate to direct his attention toward anything but me. "You remember Gretchen from Sutton, right?"

Gretchen wiggles her fingers in a wave, her lips lifting in a wicked smile as she assesses his broad frame from head to toe. "Eden was right. You *are* even taller than you were back in college. More muscular too."

Forget turning red, my face feels like it's moments away from lighting on fire. I knew I couldn't trust this girl around Holt, and right now, I could push her over the glass railing for that comment.

But Holt just chuckles, pushing his fingers through his cropped chestnut-brown hair as his gray eyes meet mine again. His voice is low, gritty, and suggestive as he says, "So, you've been talking about me, huh?"

Yup, it's official. I need to disappear right this second.

"Well, I'm going to go grab some food." I trip over my words, frantically searching for an escape route out of this conversation.

Gretchen lifts one dark brow. "I thought you said you were too nervous to eat."

If ever there was a time I needed her to close that big mouth of hers, it's right now.

I grit my teeth, forcing a smile and rattling off some excuse about feeling better now that the game has begun. I don't even fully process the words I'm saying. I'm too busy slipping hopelessly into Holt's stormy eyes. If I don't get away soon, I might drown in them.

Flustered, I excuse myself, hurrying across the suite to grab the first bacon-wrapped snack I see and popping it between my lips. Yes, my stomach is still in knots, but I'll do anything to look occupied right now. Especially if it means my mouth is too full to say anything stupid.

The taste of maple rushes over my tongue, then gives way to something not so familiar. Rubbery, almost? I tilt my head, trying to place the flavor as I slowly chew the buttery substance, letting it melt on my tongue. Which, the more I think about it, is starting to tingle a bit.

Since when is bacon spicy?

I look up to see one of the caterers smiling at me. "Enjoying the bacon-wrapped scallops?"

Scallops? Oh dear God. No.

Frantic, I snatch up a cocktail napkin, spitting the partially chewed food into it. But it's too late. My tongue has already begun to swell, filling my mouth with a fiery, itchy sensation.

The caterer's brow furrows. "Are you all right, Ms. Wynn?"

"No," I choke out, panic rising in my throat. "I'm allergic to shellfish."

10

HOLT

"Are you okay?"

"I'm all right," Eden says from beside me.

Her voice sounds slightly high-pitched, and I can tell she's more affected than she initially let on by this allergic reaction in the middle of the first game. But as the guy in charge of taking care of her, this is all in a night's work.

I would do anything to make sure she's safe—including rushing her to the nearest emergency room at nine o'clock on a Thursday night. She was so adamant at first that she was fine. But her tongue started to swell, and she admitted her throat was itchy.

Les and Gretchen helped me talk her into going to the ER out of an abundance of caution. And while she wasn't initially happy with the idea, Eden finally agreed during the first intermission. I know she doesn't want to miss the game, or cause any more of a commotion than she already has, but her health and safety will always come first.

When I give her another look, she waves me off. "Seriously. I'll be fine."

"What's your favorite kind of music?" I ask.

Eden taps her knee nervously in the passenger seat beside me. "I don't care. Just put anything on."

I look over and give her a smirk. "I'm just trying to distract you, trying to keep you talking."

She meets my eyes with a soft look. "Oh, right. Okay. I guess I'll play along."

"Perfect. Favorite music?" I ask again.

"Rock," she says, her eyebrows pushing together. "Classic or grunge. Nineties, preferably. It's such an underrated decade in terms of music."

"You think so?"

"Absolutely. I mean, the Smashing Pumpkins. Fuel. Oasis. Nirvana."

I nod. "I went through a big Incubus phase."

She laughs. "You?"

It's the first time I've heard her laugh since this whole ordeal began. And I really like the sound of it.

"I like nineties too." I turn the radio on, and since it's connected to my Bluetooth playlist, I scroll through the list of bands until I land on Incubus. "This okay?"

She nods. "Yeah."

I select the song "Drive" and press PLAY.

She looks over at me and smiles. Between that gorgeous smile that I don't deserve, and the familiar lyrics now coming from the speakers, there's a sudden ache in my chest.

Whatever tomorrow brings . . . I'll be there with open arms and open eyes.

Eden taps her knee along with the rhythm, seemingly unaware of what these words mean to me.

What I don't tell her is that the song "Wish You Were Here" was one I played on constant repeat after she bolted from my bed and my life. But I'm not brave enough to play it for her now.

When the next song comes on, "Pardon Me,"

the lyrics grab me by the throat the same way they did back then, deep in the despair of letting a girl like Eden slip through my fingers and right into the arms of a colossal dickwad. Namely, Alex Braun. That was what killed me. I knew I wasn't good enough for her. But a douchebag like him supposedly was?

Soon, those heartfelt lyrics were replaced by angrier ones, and bands like Rage Against the Machine took over my playlist.

It's quiet in my car, and I'm aware of every little thing. The way Eden's petite frame fits into the seat beside mine. Her fingers between her knees. The floral scent on her skin. The way the air seems charged between us.

"How are you feeling? We're almost there."

"I'll be fine. Throat feels a little scratchy."

"Hang in there for me." I place my hand on her knee and give it a reassuring squeeze. I wish I wasn't, but I'm all too aware of how warm her skin feels through her jeans, and how long it's been since I've touched her.

Pulling my hand away, I clear my throat. Eden seems unaffected, staring straight ahead out the windshield.

Get it together, Rossi.

When we arrive at the hospital, the check-in process is brief, and then we're waiting together in the exam room. Eden doesn't say much. She just stares at a poster of a thyroid gland on the wall. I have no idea what she's thinking, and even less of a clue about what to say to her.

It doesn't take long for them to administer an injection of epinephrine. I hold her hand, and when the nurse assumes I'm her boyfriend, neither Eden nor I correct her. After being given a packet of anti-histamines to take home for the hives on her chest, Eden signs some paperwork, and then we're strolling back through the exit less than an hour later.

"Are you okay?" I ask.

"I'm so sorry about all of this. What a mess." She shakes her head, looking down at her feet.

Not wanting her to feel ashamed, I touch her shoulders, turning her body toward mine in the parking lot. "Hey. This isn't your fault."

She bites her lip. "It's a little bit my fault. If I hadn't been so flustered, I would have paid attention to what I was putting in my mouth."

Neither of us brings up the topic that had her flustered—Eden and her friend had been gossiping about me. But it would be a dick move to press her right now. She's obviously upset.

When we reach my car, she grabs her phone, which she forgot in our rush to get into the hospital. She checks the score right away and turns to me with a smile. "We're up three to two. Four minutes left in the game."

"Nice." I nod.

When I start the car, it takes me a minute to find the sports station, but when I do, we sit in the parking lot, listening to the remaining three and a half minutes of the game. In the end, the Titans win it.

"Congrats," I say, giving Eden a grin. "How does it feel to own a winning hockey team?"

She chuckles. "I feel pretty damn good right now."

"As you should." I pull out into traffic, which is heavy because the arena is only a few blocks away. "Is your car at the arena?"

"No, I rode with Gretchen."

"I'm happy to take you home."

Eden meets my eyes with a look of gratitude. "That would be great."

She sends and receives a few congratulatory

texts as I drive. The jealous part of me wonders if she still texts with Alex, but the smarter, more rational part of me reminds me that it's none of my damn business who she texts with. Hell, maybe she's still fucking him on the side. Even then, it wouldn't be any of my concern. Eden is a gorgeous, successful woman. Of course she doesn't lack for male suitors.

I drive back to her building, which isn't far, and Eden instructs me about where to park.

"You can stop here. I'll just hop out."

I shake my head. "I'm walking you up."

She doesn't say anything further, just waits patiently for me to find parking nearby. Once I do, we head side by side into the building with its grand lobby and row of shiny silver elevators. She lives in a midrise building of luxury condos that exceed my budget by several million dollars. The location is prime, and the views are outstanding.

She unlocks the door and lets us in, setting her purse on the entryway table and flipping on lights as she moves farther inside.

The place is quiet and dark, except for the streetlights glittering from the windows a few stories below. It's nothing at all like the last time I was here, when the room was filled with testosterone and loud hockey players. Now it's just me and her—a scenario I like much better.

Am I intimidated by Eden's job, or the fact she's constantly surrounded by some of the world's most eligible men? No. Not really, anyway.

Her place is cozy and modern with wide-planked wood floors and dark gray cabinetry. The huge dark-paned windows are framed by white linen curtains. Not a thing is out of place. There's not so much as a coffee cup in the sink. It makes me wonder if she's super-neat and tidy, or if maybe she has a cleaning crew on retainer.

I bring her a glass of water from the kitchen, and she swallows one of the antihistamines.

"I'm so relieved we won tonight," she says, setting her phone on the charging tray on her kitchen counter. "It almost makes me forget about my blunder earlier."

Her eyes stay on mine as I move closer to her. When I stop directly in front of her and tip her chin toward mine, her lips part.

"You look better. Your coloring has returned, and the swelling has gone down."

"I feel fine now," she says softly.

Her gaze lowers to my mouth, just briefly, but

it's impossible to miss the look of longing in her eyes. And I can't exactly forget about what Eden and her friend had said about me . . . something about me being *hot*.

It's sure as fuck getting hot in here now.

Because while I should leave, it's the last thing in the world I want to do. What I want to do is kiss her. I want to see if we still have that same magic chemistry we had all those years ago.

The memory of her that night comes rushing back with such force and clarity, it almost knocks me over. The way she looked on my bed. How eager she seemed about everything—it ate at me. And it still does.

An onslaught of memories of what happened that night hits me hard. Maybe because it's late and we're alone together now . . . or maybe it's because Eden's bed can't be more than two dozen steps away.

Her gaze lowers to my mouth again, and I take a step back, putting some distance between us.

"I'd better go." My voice comes out rough, slightly uneven.

"That's probably a good idea," she says, sounding as shaky as I feel. "Thank you for taking me to the hospital and staying with me."

"You're very welcome," I say softly.

"Good night, Holt."

"Good night, Eden."

I let myself out and head to the elevator, releasing a long, slow sigh as my legs carry me down the hall.

All week I told myself I was imagining things. Her asking if I was single was merely job-related. The way my body reacted to seeing her? Just a product of the years between us. I kept trying to convince myself there are perfectly reasonable explanations for all of it.

Now, though? The question of am I attracted to Eden is no longer one I can deny. In fact, that question mark has been replaced with an exclamation point.

But am I man enough to go down that road again? Especially when there's so much riding on this?

That remains to be seen.

11

EDEN

Just after lunch, my phone chimes with a text.

I almost don't pick it up. I planned to spend the afternoon packing for our first away game in Detroit, considering my flight leaves in three short hours and I've done nothing but throw a pair of heels into my weekend bag so far.

But things don't always go as planned, and the second text makes me grab for my phone with a sigh. It's Gretchen, and I remember now that she texted me last night too. There's a couple of messages from her.

You okay?

Hello?

I'm coming over.

I quickly type out a reply. I'm good, you're welcome to come over. I'm packing.

A short while later, I open my front door and am greeted by a relieved-looking Gretchen holding a beverage carrier containing two extra-large coffee cups.

"Jesus, thank God your lips are back to normal size." She sighs, pressing a hand to her heart in relief. "I was afraid I was going to have to get fillers just to make you appear normal."

Before I can call her out for being overdramatic, she hands over one of the coffee cups, the one with OAT-MILK LATTE + EXTRA SHOT OF ESPRESSO scribbled in black ink on the side. Despite the amount of grief she gives me for my caffeine habit, this woman always seems to have my back.

"Sorry. After we left the emergency room, I was pretty focused on catching up on the game." I sip my latte, letting the caffeine bring me back to life. "Come help me pack for my flight?"

We head to my bedroom, where I set my coffee on the dresser to cool, turning my attention to which of my blazers screams *girl boss* the most. Meanwhile, Gretchen makes herself at home on my bed, drinking what I suspect is decaffeinated tea and surveying my mostly empty suitcase.

"So? Are you okay? Is your phone broken, or are you allergic to texting people back now too?"

"I'm fine. My throat is still a bit sore, but it's nothing." I pinch a piece of lint off a navy-blue cowl-neck sweater, then fold it neatly and drop it into my suitcase. "And I'm sorry for not texting you back. Between the hospital visit and then getting home late . . . my mind was occupied."

"Yeah? With Holt?"

I roll my eyes to keep her from reading me like a well-worn playbook. Gretchen knows me well enough to spot that flicker in my eyes that I get at just the mention of a guy I'm interested in. "No, not with Holt. Just, ya know, with getting an EpiPen stabbed into my thigh."

She gives me a wry smile. "Right, while Holt was holding your hand."

Suddenly, packing seems like the least important thing in the world. My gaze returns to Gretchen in a panic. "How did you know that? It's not on the hockey blogs, is it?"

My memory races back to the night before. Could one of the nurses be part of some whisper-network of hockey fans, ratting me out to the blogosphere for holding my security guard's hand? Can't a woman having an allergic reaction seek a little emotional support?

"Uh, I *didn't* know that," Gretchen says slowly. "And neither do the blogs. I was making a joke. But now that you've said that, I'm extra glad I came over to gossip." She grins.

Relief courses through my veins, followed immediately by defeat. I'm not going to be able to avoid talking about this with her.

Gretchen reclines into my heap of throw pillows and blows on her tea. She tries a sip and grimaces to find it's still too hot. "Spill, girl. What happened last night?"

"Nothing," I say curtly. It's the truth.

She frowns. "You're lying."

"No, I'm not. Nothing happened. I mean, he walked me up to my apartment, and there was definitely, you know, some chemistry. But neither of us acted on it. And why would we after I made such a colossal ass of myself?"

"Having an allergic reaction is not the same as making an ass of yourself."

"Maybe. But hacking up half-chewed food into

a napkin after implying that your security detail is hot? I think that sort of qualifies." I grab my latte again, popping the lid off to temporarily hide behind the billowing steam.

"For the record, *I'm* the one who implied he was hot," Gretchen says, correcting me. "Which he is. And it could've been worse. You could have thrown up on him. You've got to look on the bright side here."

"There is no bright side. There's only one side to this whole situation. The deeply confusing side."

Flustered, I sit on the edge of my bed, taking a big, well-deserved sip of my latte. It burns my tongue a little, but I hardly notice. It's nothing compared to how swollen and tingly it was last night, so there's that.

"What's so confusing? You're doing great. Your team won last night. They're going to crush it again tonight. And you've got a sexy-as-fuck bodyguard who follows you around."

I let out a shaky sigh. "It's just a lot to handle. The games, the gossip, the fact that this city still isn't on my side. Alex. Toss in Holt on top of it, and I just . . ." I shudder, letting myself feel everything at once.

I never had that ride-or-die tribe of women

in college that others seemed to have. Yes, I had Gretchen, but she and I weren't *that* close. She has a group of girlfriends that she's had since high school and often hung out with them.

I tried not to let that bother me, but to be honest, sometimes it did. My social media feed made it seem that every other female out there had this pack of girlfriends who were there through every triumph and failure. But after my very public breakup and subsequent promotion, I barely got two or three phone calls from friends asking how I was doing.

Of course, one was Gretchen, but I just never had that big group of friends. I guess that suits me. I'm more of a loner than I let on. But that doesn't mean I don't long for more close friendships.

And don't even get me started on the mess of confusion that is Holt. He's always made me feel a lot of things. Attraction. Fascination. Anxiety.

I throw up my hands, forgetting for a moment that I'm still holding my latte and almost spill it all over my white duvet.

Frustrated, I leap to my feet. "See? I'm a shit show."

"Okay, let's break this down. One thing at a time." Gretchen's expression has turned serious.

"Alex? I thought we were past that."

"We are," I say with certainty. "Doesn't mean it's not hard seeing him all the freaking time."

She gives me a pensive look, as if trying to work out my feelings. "Okay . . ." The word leaves her lips slowly and with uncertainty.

Gretchen clearly doesn't understand why this has been so hard for me. She knows I've moved on, and I really have. I don't want another shot with Alex. I've been there, done that, given him my whole heart, and it still didn't work out. She was right that I've moved on, but someone who hasn't worked with their ex will never understand the struggle. It's really a top-notch experience. Well done.

Blah. I feel like banging my head against the wall repeatedly. Thankfully, I don't. I do, however, grab a set of gray cotton pajamas and toss them inside my bag.

"And then there's Holt," she says cautiously but with a flirtatious tilt to her mouth. "They're so different in every way."

You can say that again.

"There's nothing between me and Holt other than some lingering chemistry." Even as I say the words, I wonder if they're true.

"If you say so." Her tone is filled with doubt.

To hear Gretchen question my motives, when it comes to a man who I myself admittedly don't understand, leaves me feeling vulnerable. It's jarring.

"There's been nothing between you two since you fled his bed that morning?"

"Not since that walk of shame."

She huffs. "I told you I don't like that term. It's not a walk of shame. It's a stride of pride."

This pulls a chuckle out of me.

The conversation moves on, and when I glance over at her, instead of pity in Gretchen's eyes, she's suppressing a laugh.

I plant my hands on my hips, tilting my chin at her. "What?"

"You know what you need?"

"A chill pill?" I'm only half joking, but she shakes her head.

"No, you need to bang Holt to get him out of your system. You robbed yourself of that back in college, and that feeling of loss has lingered."

Yeah, right.

I scoff, waving off her comment. "No way is that going to happen."

"I'm totally serious." Her tone is insistent and less playful than it was before. "I think it's the only way you're going to stop being so tightly wound about the whole thing."

As I finish the last of my packing, I weigh the idea carefully. The thought hasn't occurred to me before, but now that it's out there, it sticks in my brain more than I care to admit.

Would it really be possible for me to climb into Holt's bed again, just to make my same escape before we got carried away? Maybe we do just need to finish what we started so many years ago. It's possible that's true—before I can truly turn the page on that chapter of my life.

Or maybe I'm delusional, and the press would run wild with it. If the media thought I was sleeping my way through the team—security, staff, players, whoever—it could ruin everything. One blog post could bring me to my knees.

And not in the fun, sexy way.

No, it would be a total embarrassment. I'm stronger than that. Smarter. I have to be.

"No, Gretchen." I shake my head. "You know that's not possible. You saw all the news articles condemning me before I even started this job. People assume I'm going to melt down over my ex, or fall onto some other player's stick. Holt might not be a Titan, but he's still employed by the team. I can't let them be right."

I throw one last comfy sleep shirt into my bag, then zip it up. It's closed, just like this topic.

Gretchen nods as she takes the tiniest sip of her tea. "So, what are you going to do?"

My mouth lifts in a slight smile. "My job, first and foremost. But more immediately? I'm going to go to the airport, fly to Detroit, and watch the Titans kick some ass."

12

HOLT

This is it. Our first trip for an away game.

When I board the team's private jet, I have a surreal moment, wondering if this is actually my reality. As head of security, I've traveled with clients before, and I've flown on private jets more upscale than this one. Still, the fact that I'm traveling with a professional sports team—an experience that most fans would give their left nut for—isn't lost on me. Too bad I'm not a hockey fan in the slightest.

Eden is in the second row seated next to her assistant, Aspen, and they're deep in conversation. Les is in the row across from them. I step into the aisle and keep my eyes straight ahead—toward the back of the plane.

Clusters of players are spread out in the seats,

some shuffling cards, and others pretending to sleep. The goalie, a French-Canadian guy named Lucian, watches a movie on his tablet as I pass.

I take an empty seat near the middle of the plane and pull out my phone to send a text to Eden. Are you doing okay?

I wait for a couple of minutes, but she doesn't reply. Maybe her phone is already set to airplane mode. And since we're getting ready to take off, I do the same.

As we find our cruising altitude, I can't help but overhear a few of the guys talking about a certain dating app and arranging hookups at the hotel. Alex Braun laughs along to the conversation and doesn't dispute that he'll be doing this too.

If he does anything to humiliate or embarrass Eden, I will fucking end him. Hasn't he put her through enough? I can't even look at him, with his easy smile and cocky playboy attitude.

"You're Holt, right?" someone asks from behind me.

I turn in my seat and find one of the defensemen, Price St. James, known to his teammates as Saint, looking at me. "Yeah. That's me."

He nods. "Is everything going okay? With

Eden, I mean."

"I'm not sure what you mean," I say, not sure if he heard about the shellfish incident last night.

"She's not like getting," he lowers his voice, "death threats, is she?"

So maybe he hasn't heard about her allergic reaction after all. He seems more interested in my presence and why she's now traveling with extra security.

I shake my head. "No, nothing like that. Just some loudmouthed fans calling for her resignation. I'm here as a precaution."

Saint nods, stretching his long legs out in front of him. "They're wrong. She's going to be a great owner. I can tell."

"You should tell her so."

"You think?" His mouth lifts in an uncertain smile.

I nod. "You know what they say . . . it's lonely at the top. She may appreciate hearing something positive once in a while."

"Yeah, good point." Saint rubs at the stubble on his jaw. "I'll do that."

I give him a polite smile, wondering if he's single and wants more from Eden than he's letting on.

Jeez, drop it, Rossi.

Not every guy on this team wants to fuck her. Probably not, anyway. I mean . . . Lucian's married, and there are rumors that Lindquist is gay.

Man, I'm really losing it.

I shove my earbuds into my ears and crank up my music, trying to tune out my own tumultuous thoughts. It doesn't work, and I spend the flight feeling agitated.

• • •

Two hours later, we've landed and deplaned in Detroit. It's colder than I expected, and the sky is gray. It's not exactly a warm welcome.

I catch up to Eden on the tarmac as everyone waits to board the bus that will take us to the hotel. She's dressed in a sleek black coat and carrying a large leather purse.

"How are you feeling?" I ask.

She smiles at my concern. "I'm fine. Thank you."

"Did you have a good flight?"

She nods. "I did. I wanted to nap, but instead Aspen and I mapped out some work I want to do on an upcoming charity campaign this holiday season."

"That's good."

She nods.

I can feel her assistant, Aspen, watching us. Something between Eden and me feels strained, and I have no idea why.

"Any plans tonight?" I ask, taking my turn to board the bus.

Eden sits down in the seat behind me. "Not really. I'm sure some of the guys will go out to dinner, but I'm kind of tired, honestly. I'll probably just stay in. Maybe take a bath, order some room service, and turn in early."

When I meet her eyes, I can guess at what she isn't saying. She's nervous—about the game, most likely. Or maybe about being alone with me again. But that can't be true, can it? I'm probably only imagining the chemistry between us.

"Okay, well, if you need anything, I'm in the room next to yours," I say, giving her one last look before I face forward again.

She doesn't say anything else.

At the hotel, I escort Eden to her room and then let myself into mine, which is right next door. I glance in her direction as she uses the keycard to unlock her door. "Well, enjoy."

I try to sound nonchalant, but inside I'm as *chalant* as fuck. I don't know what's happening to me, but I feel so on edge, I could burst. Since I'm not needed, but there's no way I can relax, I change into my gym clothes and decide to hit the hotel's workout facility, which is two floors down.

I don't even feel like working out. My heart's not in it, but I need to clear my head. Need to blow off some steam, and it's either fuck something—*hard*—or run and lift weights. So I obviously do the latter.

I crank up the pace on the treadmill while loud, angry music blares in my ears.

I've been fighting with myself for days, ever since I came back into Eden's life. Fighting to remind myself of all the things that I can never have, Eden included.

After thirty minutes on the treadmill, now breathless and sweaty, I move over to the free weights. The gym leaves a lot to be desired, especially after I've become so spoiled with the team's training facility. But still, it does the job. As I bang out set after set of bicep curls, my mind wanders.

Of course it wanders straight to a certain five-foot-something powerhouse who totally blew me off earlier. I'm not sure why her brush-off should feel so significant. Maybe it's because I've been down this road before.

Just as I finish up one last set of shoulder presses, my phone buzzes with a text. I pick it up and glance at it.

It's Eden, and my heart jumps.

Can we talk?

13

EDEN

Nerves fill my stomach as I wait for Holt's reply. But I shouldn't have been worried, because it comes less than ten seconds later.

Sure.

It's only one word, but now I'm nervous for an entirely different reason.

I type out in reply, Come by my room.

Aspen put me in a hotel room right next to Holt's, in case I needed him for security reasons at a moment's notice. And a few minutes later, there's a knock.

When I tug the door open, it certainly seems

like I caught him in the middle of a moment. His hair is dripping wet, like my text might have interrupted his shower, and his not-quite-towel-dried body makes his fitted charcoal V-neck cling even tighter to his chest.

"Everything okay?" he asks, his gray eyes clouded with concern.

"Yes, I'm fine. Sorry, I know it's late." I step back from the doorway, and he joins me inside. "Have you eaten dinner yet?"

"Not yet. I just finished working out. Well, actually, I just finished a shower, but before that I was squeezing in a workout."

As he talks, he works one hand through his damp hair, allowing me to catch the slightest whiff of mint and eucalyptus. Definitely the hotel bodywash. It's a change from his usual woodsy, earthy scent, and I can't help but admire the way his biceps flex as he tries to air-dry his hair with his hands.

Focus, Eden. You didn't invite him over for dinner and a show. There are actual conversations to be had.

"We should order food," I say, tilting my chin toward the menu on my nightstand. "I was too nervous to eat earlier, so I took a bubble bath to calm down instead."

His stormy gaze momentarily dips from mine to assess the fluffy white hotel robe I'm still wearing. "Did it work?"

"Sadly, no. I'm still as on edge as ever." I tug the terrycloth belt a little tighter, staring down with embarrassment at the hotel slippers on my feet. Had I known he would be over in such a hurry, I would have gotten properly dressed.

But when I look back up at Holt, he's not smirking at my appearance like I would expect. Instead, a shallow crease has formed across his forehead. He's studying me with a sort of intensity that might feel somewhat off-putting coming from anyone else, but there's something oddly comforting about having Holt look at me this way, like I'm a puzzle he's trying to solve.

"So, is that why you texted me then?" he finally asks, one brow quirking upward. "To help take the edge off?"

His phrasing sends the slightest tingle of electricity radiating from my chest to my fingertips. I can think of one very effective way he could help me take the edge off, a method that I'm certain Gretchen would approve of.

How did she phrase it again? I should *get him out of my system*, or something like that?

Whatever it was, it's not the reason I invited him over tonight. In fact, it's not even an option at all. Not tonight, and not ever. I need to shake that possibility for good.

"I just need to talk through some things," I say, folding my arms over my chest. "But let's order food first. I could use dinner. And maybe a glass of wine."

Yes, definitely wine, I decide in that moment. Although I seldom drink during the week, I'll make an exception tonight.

With a quick nod, Holt sits on the edge of my bed and grabs the menu for the hotel restaurant, reading the options aloud—burgers, salads, typical hotel fare. I settle on a club sandwich, and he calls our order in, tacking on a bison burger for himself and a bottle of rosé.

"Thank God for room service," I mutter.

Despite my instinct to sit next to him on the bed, I opt for the plush cream-colored sofa across the room. I tuck one ankle behind the other, focusing on keeping my knees glued together. It's the only way to distract myself from those hypnotic gray eyes.

"So," he says, planting his elbows on his knees and leaning toward me. It's the same position Coach Wilder assumes when he's talking to the players in the locker room. "What's got you so stressed?"

I fuss with the belt of my robe, avoiding eye contact. "Is *everything* an acceptable answer? I'm just so worried about the team."

Without even looking up, I can feel Holt's warm gaze on me as he waits patiently for me to say more.

Well. Here goes.

"Aspen gave me the full download on our flight here," I say, pressing to my feet and beginning to pace. "The blogs are saying last night's win was a fluke, more of a sign that the opposing team needs work than anything else. They picked our offensive line apart, insisting that we're doomed, and Lord knows that I'll be the one to blame for a losing season."

"It's not exclusively your responsibility," he says, but I'm too wrapped up in my own downward spiral to acknowledge his comment.

"What if I can't handle this? What if I let my grandpa, my whole family, everyone down? What if I run the entire Titans franchise into the ground till it's worth nothing and I have to walk away with my tail between my legs?"

I slow to a stop, heaving a sigh as I will my anxious heart rate back to a normal speed. That was . . . more than I planned on saying. When I've caught my breath, I turn back toward Holt, who is staring at the calluses on his palms, nodding slowly as he processes my word vomit.

Frustrated, I huff out, "Say something."

He meets my eyes, and there's something solemn about his expression. Finally, he speaks.

"I have an idea. Wait here."

Before I can say another word, he shoves up from the bed and stalks toward the door, flipping the latch before he leaves to keep it from locking behind him. And just as quickly as he arrived, he's gone.

My heart squeezes. What happened? Did my oversharing scare him off?

Before I can assemble a complete catalog of worst-case scenarios, he reappears in my doorway, gripping a well-read paperback book.

"What's that?"

"My therapist gave it to me," he says, turning it over in his hands. "*Seabiscuit*. She thought it might help me if I read it."

"Did you?"

He shrugs. "I got through some of it."

"And did it help?"

"I don't know. It's about these three guys who team up to help make this horse—Seabiscuit, that was an underdog, a horse no one thought could win—into a champion."

"I'm familiar with the gist of it," I say, recalling seeing the movie many years ago. "But why did your therapist recommend it?"

I'm also curious about why he sees a therapist, but that conversation feels a bit too heavy for a moment like this. He's already exposing part of himself in offering me the book. Just knowing he's trying to help—well, it makes me sympathetic.

Holt blows out a sigh, rubbing his palm along the stubble on his jaw. It makes a soft, scratching sound that I know I'll be thinking about for the rest of the night.

"She said I had to let more people in. Not be so self-reliant. You know, like the guys in the book. It takes all three of them to get the job done." He stares down at the cover, flipping through the pages for a long moment before finally meeting my gaze.

"So, did you?" I ask. "Let more people in, that

is?"

The smallest smirk forms on his lips. "Not really, no."

I can't help but laugh. "At least you're honest."

When he passes the book to me, I run my thumb along the well-worn spine, inspecting the back cover. "So, what are you saying?"

"I guess I'm saying that you don't have to do everything yourself. It's up to the entire organization. The coaching staff. The players. It's up to the marketing department. Up to the fans to show up. You have to rely on them. If you fail, you fail together."

A nervous chuckle escapes me. "How comforting."

"The point is, the only thing you can control is your own actions," he says, his voice gentle. "Control what you can and let go of what you can't. Trust your team to do their part."

It's quiet between us, a comfortable silence in which we do nothing but stare into each other's eyes. His are so expressive, clouding and clearing as his mood shifts. Right now, they're a soft gray, the color of an old comfy sweatshirt I used to have back in my Sutton days.

Everything about Holt is like a perfectly preserved memory that I'm desperate to slip back into, just like that sweatshirt. Even though my brain is constantly screaming at me to be professional, my body has other ideas. He's just so handsome. And protective of me. That combination is dangerous and really does something to a girl.

"I was worried about you, you know," he says, his voice barely above a whisper. "After the emergency room visit."

I slouch back into my seat, folding my arms over my chest. "I was fine."

"I texted you," he says. "On the plane. You never responded."

"I know," I whisper to the floor. "I'm sorry."

More silence, and this time, it's not so comfortable. It's heavy with all the unspoken words that are begging to be said, the ones we're both avoiding. But if ever there was a time to be vulnerable with him, it has to be now.

I move from the couch to the spot next to him on the bed, close enough to breathe in the scent of mint and eucalyptus and man. "Can I admit something to you? Something not work-related?"

"Anything, Eden."

I swallow hard, hoping he really means that. Because I think part of why I'm so twisted up inside is because of this man right here.

"I haven't really been able to stop thinking about that night we shared," I admit on a whisper, steadying my gaze on the hotel logo on my slippers.

I pause, turning back to assess his reaction, but he's silent, his soft eyes attentive. I'm hoping he'll say something in return, but when he doesn't, I resort to rambling, desperate to fill the quiet.

"I know it's crazy and it was so long ago, and we were practically teenagers back in those days, but I just can't—"

Holt doesn't give me the chance to finish that thought. Instead, with a shift of his weight on the bed, he closes the short distance between us, breaking every invisible boundary with one press of his full lips against mine.

One kiss. That's all it takes for me to throw every doubt, every rule I've set for myself, out the window.

In this moment, I curse my twenty-one-year-old self for ever leaving this man's bed. Because the way he kisses me—gently, deeply, sweeter than I've ever been kissed before—is something I never want to run away from.

He sucks gently at my lower lip, running his tongue along it and sending a rush of endorphins surging through my system, the kind that make me act against my better judgment. Suddenly, my hands are gripping his shoulders, pulling him in until we're toppling back, his body moving over mine in a slow, greedy grind.

"We shouldn't be doing this," he murmurs against my throat. By the way he trails wet, open-mouthed kisses down to my collarbone, though, he's showing no signs of slowing down.

"Do you want to stop?" I ask breathlessly.

"Fuck no."

I can feel his smile against my skin as he nips gently at my jawline, spurring a gasp to fall from my lips. He chuckles, and a flutter beats in my chest at the sound.

God, that laugh. It could bring a woman to her knees. It has before, in fact, and it might again.

"Maybe just this once?" I say, my voice small but hopeful. We've done this before. Sort of. What's once more?

But instead of his low, rich voice in reply, a different voice answers. A soft, feminine voice from outside the door.

"Room service."

My stomach leaps into my throat as I shoot up in bed, pushing Holt as far away from me as possible.

Holy awkward.

"Don't worry, I've got it," he reassures me, rearranging himself in his joggers before heading for the door.

A young dark-haired woman dressed in black smiles as she wheels in a silver cart, oblivious to the situation she just interrupted.

Meanwhile, I'm trying to make myself as small as possible on the bed, hoping my robe will let me blend in with the white duvet. Once our food is set up, Holt slips the girl a few bills from his wallet, thanking her before locking the door behind her.

"So, uh . . ." He shoves his hands into his pockets, smiling at me shyly. "I guess we should eat?"

After a long pause, I burst out laughing and Holt grins, and all the tension in the room dissipates. Even the most awkward moments are made a little bit better by his presence.

With the awkwardness out of the way, we relocate to the small table in the corner and digging in. Between bites, we talk about music, and he sends me the playlist he had on in the car the other day, making me promise to listen to it before the game tomorrow.

"It'll hype you up," he says, muscling the cork out of our bottle of rosé. "I promise."

Once our glasses are filled, I lift mine in the air, arching a brow in his direction. "What should we toast to?"

"To letting people in," he says with a smile, and before I can agree, he clinks his glass against mine, making it official.

The wine goes down smooth and easy. A little too easy, maybe, because after a lively debate about which nineties bands are the best, we've both finished our glasses.

Holt listens to me talk about the team, to my ramblings about save percentages, goals, and assists, then listens when I complain about the sports commentator who seems to have it in for me. And he grins when I help myself to a little more wine and say *fuck it* to all of that.

This is the most laid-back I've seen him since, well, ever, and his calming energy has had quite the effect on me. The wine probably helps, but I shouldn't have any more. One last sip, and I set my glass aside.

"Are you done?" he asks.

I nod, eyeing the wineglass. "I think so."

"Finish it."

"We have a big day tomorrow, remember?" I shake my head. "And you're way bigger than me. Your tolerance is higher. You finish it."

He lifts the glass and eyeballs what's left in it, swirling the light pink liquid around. "If I do, can I kiss you again?"

My heart squeezes. Doesn't he already know the answer? "You can kiss me again either way."

With a grin, he takes a sip from my glass and then offers it to me. I take one last swallow and he sets the glass aside.

Moments later, he's guiding me up from my chair, his big hands lifting me by the hips into the air. I squeal, and we land on the sofa, where just an hour ago, I sat to keep my distance from him. Now, distance is the last thing on my mind.

His lips find mine again, more desperate and eager than before, his tongue moving over mine in hot, hungry strokes. I grip his shoulders, moaning into his mouth as his hands venture down the front of my robe in search of my belt.

"Can I?" he asks, his voice raspy with need.

I nod, and he tugs the knot loose, unwrapping me slowly, like a fine piece of chocolate he wants to savor. It's been too long since I've been naked with someone, much longer since that someone has looked at me this way, his wild eyes drinking in every inch of my skin.

I'm not wearing any makeup, and my hair is damp on the ends from the tub, but it doesn't matter. The way Holt looks at me... this is the sexiest I've ever felt. When he sinks to his knees, my breath catches as his palms run gently up my thighs.

Good God in heaven, this is really happening.

A hot, ragged breath pours from his lips, warming my core and commanding every nerve ending in my body to stand alert. When I finally dare to look down at him, he's looking up at me, eager to solve the puzzle in my eyes again. Only this time, there's nothing to solve.

I want him. I need him. And if he doesn't touch me right this second, I'm going to shatter into a thousand tiny pieces.

"We can stop if you want," he whispers, pressing a kiss into my inner thigh, the scruff of his jaw scratching gently against my sensitive skin.

But he's wrong. You can't stop a storm once the clouds start gathering. You can't stop a wave from breaking once it's crashing toward the shore. And I can't—I *refuse* to—keep us apart tonight. Not when he's so painfully close to the neediest part of me. Not when I want him this much.

"Like hell we can." Panting, I grip the back of his head and guide him right to where I want him.

His warm lips find my clit, and I release the strangled moan I've barely been holding back. *Ho. Ly. Fuck.*

My head falls back against the couch as his expert mouth works me over, sucking and licking in ways that make my whole body quiver. My hands grapple for a solid grip on the couch cushions but eventually land on his shoulders.

"God, Holt," I say on a ragged breath. "I'm so close."

No sooner have the words left my lips than my orgasm rips through me in hot, pulsating waves. It takes me a long while to come down from my high, almost a full minute before I can manage a single word.

"Shit."

He snickers softly, joining me back on the couch and running his big hand along my thigh. I instantly spot the stiffness in his joggers, which he doesn't bother trying to hide.

Looping a thumb into his waistband, I press a kiss to his lips. "Mind if I return the favor?"

"Only if you want," he says, tipping my chin up so his gentle eyes can meet mine, and I can see just how much he means every word. "We don't have to do anything more than you're comfortable with. Just like last time."

"And just like last time, I want you." I sweep a finger beneath his waistband, and a low hum of pleasure escapes my lips at the knowledge he skipped the boxers tonight.

"Didn't have time to put underwear on when you texted me," he says sheepishly.

"Just less to take off," I purr. "So, can I?"

"Fuck yeah."

I help him out of his joggers, centering myself on the floor between his big, parted thighs. He grips his base, giving himself a few precursory strokes, and good God, Holt has gotten bigger over the years in more ways than one.

Slowly, I replace his hand with mine, moving it just the way he taught me so many years ago. A tight grip on his base, a slow drag of my hand up his shaft up and over the tip. My memory doesn't fail me, and neither does my form, based on the way Holt groans my name.

"Jesus, Eden," he chokes out. "That's so fuck-ing good."

When I bring my mouth to his wide shaft, words fail him, and my only warning that he's close is a series of short, needy grunts. Over and over, I guide my lips to meet my hand, feeling him grow tenser and tighter until he lets out one exasperated moan, finishing in wet, hot spurts in the back of my throat.

"F-fuck," he stutters, pushing one hand through his hair as he blinks up at the ceiling.

His broad chest rises and falls quickly at first, then slower with time as he regains composure. When he finally smiles down at me, there's a stormy glint in his night-sky eyes.

"Get up here, you."

I scramble up onto the couch next to him, and he tugs his pants back up while I tie my robe again, then nestle into the crook of his shoulder. Just for a moment. Long enough to remember how well we fit together, how perfect and familiar this is. And then I force myself to say the words I so desperately don't want to say.

"You should probably go back to your room."

He dips his chin in a nod, giving my arm a quick squeeze. "Sure. We don't need anyone seeing me come out of here this late or anything."

"Exactly," I say, but there's a sadness in my voice that can't be denied.

Still, I walk him to the door, pressing onto my tiptoes to place one last kiss on his jaw before he goes.

"Thanks for the book," I whisper.

"You're welcome," he murmurs.

14

HOLT

When the team loses their game in Detroit, the only person I feel for is Eden. I couldn't give two shits about the grumpy cluster of hockey players sitting glumly in the visiting team's dressing room inside the Detroit arena.

I wonder about how *she's* doing, but she's currently meeting behind closed doors with Les, which is why I'm biding my time with the guys, when all I want to do is check on Eden. She knows as well as I do, the best way to get revenge on her vocal critics is success—which means winning games. She was so worried last night, but what I told her is the truth.

It's the players' jobs to score goals and win games. Eden's job is to run the franchise and handle the finances, something she's uniquely prepared to do, given her education and training. I'm hoping it's only a minor setback in what will end up being a very successful season for her.

Although, I can't help but wonder if what's been happening between us distracted her from her role in some way. But that couldn't be it, could it? Things last night spiraled out of control—in all the best ways—but we haven't had any time together today, so I can only imagine what she might be thinking.

Does she regret it? I feel a lot of things about last night, but regret isn't one of them.

"That Sharpe fucker needs to go down," one of the players grumbles.

Patrice Sharpe is one of the most celebrated members of Detroit's starting line. He scored twice tonight, ruining the Titans' chances for a comeback since they couldn't seem to get the puck to the net at all in the third period. It was a joke. They looked like shit. But like I said, the last thing I feel is sympathetic. Most of them are overpaid divas as far as I'm concerned.

Saint stands and tosses a damp towel in a large basket in the center of the room. "It's in the past. We've got to put it out of our heads. Got another chance tomorrow."

He isn't the captain, but as I look up and glance around the room, I can see that though he's young, he's respected by the team.

A few more thoughts are shared on their loss, but I have little interest. I watch the door on the side of the room, waiting for it to open, but it doesn't. Most of the guys have filtered out of the room. Alex Braun remains, and so do Saint and the heavily bearded Reeves. I try to focus on something on my phone, but I'm on edge and irritated.

"We can't afford to be distracted like that again," Saint says with a cocky smirk.

"You fuckers were entertaining those puck bunnies well past midnight," Reeves grumbles. "Don't think I didn't notice that."

Saint raises both hands. "That was Braun's idea."

My stomach sours.

Eden is in that room, feeling like shit—probably crying her eyes out to Les—all because Alex fucking Braun decided he needed to get laid last night and couldn't do his damn job on the ice.

Alex saunters past us, headed for the exit, freshly showered and dressed in a wrinkle-free navy-blue suit. Without thinking, I rise quickly and intercept him in the hallway, letting the heavy door thud closed behind us.

"What the—" Alex sputters as I press into his personal space.

I curse under my breath and shove one of his shoulders against the cinderblock wall. "I just overheard something about you and the guys who were *entertaining* late last night."

He glares at me. "So?"

"So, when you fuck up the game because of your extracurriculars, it catches people's attention."

"How exactly is that any of your business?" Alex gives me a shove, and I take a step back.

"Because you need to keep things discreet. And if you ever cared about Eden, you need to stop this. Word is going to get out, and you're going to ruin any chance you had at a friendship with her."

He scoffs at this. "I doubt we're on track to be besties, anyway. Pretty sure she hates me."

My fists clench at my sides, and I'm sure there's a vein throbbing in my neck. "You're going to publicly humiliate her. Be more discreet or you'll have me to deal with."

"What are you, her babysitter now?"

"No, just a friend."

He smirks, giving me a self-satisfied look. "Right. A friend who's on the payroll. Got it. Just don't forget that, Rossi." He takes a menacing step closer. "Don't forget that the only reason why she wants you around is because you're an *employee* here. You're not her friend."

His personality and mine just don't mix. We'll never see eye to eye, and that's fine with me. But if he still thinks of Eden as a toy he doesn't want anyone else to play with, we're going to have a big fucking problem. She's capable of deciding who she wants to share her time and her body with, and even if that guy isn't me, the choice is still hers. Alex holds no claim over her anymore.

I wonder then if he knows about Eden's history with me. If he suspects there's something going on between us now. But it doesn't matter. He needs to keep his nose clean and do what this league is paying him to do—which is to play hockey, not hook up with puck bunnies.

"Fuck you, Braun. Just keep your dick in your pants and don't upset Eden, or you're going to be fucking with me."

He scoffs again. "Whatever, dude. I'll fuck

with whoever I want."

I slam my palm into the wall just as Eden comes through the door and enters the hallway beside us. "Holt? Alex? What the hell is going on?" Confusion crinkles her brow.

"Nothing," I lie.

Alex shoulders his way past us, grumbling something under his breath I can't catch. We watch him stalk away until he's out of sight, and then it's just me and her. The air is still charged around us.

Eden straightens her posture, squaring her shoulders. "Don't lie to me. What's going on? Did Alex say something to you?"

I release a slow exhale as I consider my options.

I won't lie to Eden, but I don't exactly want to tell her the truth either. Because even if they're broken up, on some level his sleeping around might hurt her, and that's the last thing I want.

"I won't lie to you, so if you really need to know, I will tell you. But please just trust me."

She gives me a pleading look.

"I'll tell you if and when there's something you need to know. Okay?"

I can see the moment she gives in. Her shoulders relax. "Okay. But only because I sense you're trying to protect me from something ugly, and my life could use less stress right now, not more."

My instincts were right. Somehow they always seem to be with this woman.

I reach out for her and place one hand on her shoulder. She leans into my touch, letting me rub her neck and shoulder briefly. In that moment, I realize I'd do anything to ease her burden, anything to make her feel good and whole again.

She meets my eyes again. "I still want to know what Alex said to you."

I give her a pleased smile. She never gives up. Never backs down. It's just not in her nature. "I know you do. But remember, lions don't concern themselves with the opinions of sheep. And you are a lion. Got it?"

A shy smile tugs at her mouth, and my heart leaps. Who is this girl? She makes me feel so many messy, confusing emotions. Most of them all at once. It's disorienting.

"Got it," she says with a smile.

"Are you ready to get out of here?" I tip my chin toward the stairwell.

She nods. "Yes. And ready to be back home. The hotel bed didn't agree with me last night."

"You can come by my room tonight if you want. My bed was comfortable."

She smirks, glancing at me as we head up the stairs together. "Oh, really. You sure you wouldn't mind?"

I smile, but I don't dare touch her right now because someone could see us. "I wouldn't mind at all."

Eden plays coy, pursing her lips. "I don't know. I might just stay in tonight and read. I started this really good book someone gave me the other night."

I chuckle and shake my head.

When we reach the top of the stairs, her assistant appears with some questions, furiously typing something into a tablet. Eden gives me a look that says she's sorry to be done with our playful conversation, but I can sense that she needs to focus on work now, so I say good-bye.

"I'll see you later," I say.

"I might be able to work you in," she says, and then she winks.

My heart takes off at a gallop.

15

EDEN

As I hide in my hotel room like a coward, I can't help replaying Holt's offer from earlier over and over in my head. The way his deep voice rumbled over the words. Those words being . . . an invitation to share his bed.

I heave a sigh, falling back onto my bed and staring blankly at Holt's contact on my phone. Thus far, the texting box has remained empty. I guess I'm hoping the right words will magically fall off my thumbs.

What do you say to someone when you're looking for a booty call, but you don't want your booty call to know he's a booty call?

And now I've officially thought the words *booty call* so many times, they don't even sound like a real phrase. And is that really what Holt is? I think part of me knows he's much more than that.

With a huff, I drop my phone onto my pillow and redirect all this cagey energy toward the view out my window, like the solution to my problem might be hidden somewhere in the night sky.

Why am I letting myself get so worked up? For all I know, Holt might have been joking when he made that comment. After all, last night when we crossed that boundary, I was the one who said it was a one-time thing. Not that it's stopped my memory from replaying every moment of it.

As it turns out, Gretchen was very wrong about me getting Holt out of my system. If anything, one taste of him has only left me craving more. Every time his stormy eyes met mine today, I remembered that wicked look that danced through them moments before he proceeded to give me the best orgasm of my life.

I want to explore this thing with him, but I have no idea how to proceed with caution—especially for someone in my role with this organization. It's a virtual human resources nightmare, if I'm being honest. Nothing about this situation is smart on my part. But as I learned once long ago, sometimes good girls need to be bad.

My phone buzzes, interrupting my stargazing,

and I ready myself for an email from Aspen, or a notification from ESPN about the game. Instead, what I find makes my eyebrows shoot up, while simultaneously sparking a warm, jittery feeling in my chest.

I swipe my thumb over the notification, opening the text. Congrats on the win, BTW. Don't know if I said that before.

A smile tugs at my lips as my thumbs fly across the keyboard, firing off a reply. Thanks :) What are you still doing up? Our flight leaves early tomorrow.

Normally, protocol would dictate that one should wait a little while before responding to a text from a guy, but something about Holt has me feeling a bit more eager than usual.

Much to my surprise, he responds not with another text, but with a phone call.

Jesus. Here I was, scrutinizing every word of a potential message to him. Meanwhile, he has the guts to just call out of the blue? That's the kind of confidence I need to tap into.

After a brief, centering breath, I answer. "Hello?"

Holt's low, rough voice washes over me. "Hey. You finally done working for the night?"

My teeth sink into my lower lip. "Yes, I'm done. Were you checking up on me?" I ask quietly.

His laugh is a low chuckle on the other end of the line. "Something like that."

I drop onto the corner of the bed, and just like every time I'm with him, all the tension I've been hanging on to slips away. "Well, thanks for checking in."

"As much as I'd like to accept the accolades, this call is less professional and more personal in nature," he says somewhat shyly.

"Oh?" I ask, biting my lower lip.

"I was serious about what I said earlier. No pressure, but I'd really like to see you again."

I pick absently at a hangnail, weighing the angel on one of my shoulders against the devil on the other. I was so hung up on how to phrase a text to Holt asking if I could see him tonight, that I didn't even consider the details of that possibility.

If one of the players spotted me leaving our head of security's room in the morning, every bit of the respect I've managed to build over the past month would be as good as gone.

Then again, we pulled this off back in Detroit. Sure, our rooms were right next to each other then, but we might be able to duplicate a similar arrangement—I swing by for a bit, then leave quietly before it's late enough for anyone to get suspicious.

"Eden? Are you there?"

"Mm-hmm," I murmur, drumming my fingers against my thigh. "Just figuring out logistics. Maybe I can just stop by for a little while?"

"Sounds good. Room sixteen fourteen."

"Perfect," I whisper. It's three doors down from mine. "See you soon."

Pressing to my feet, I inspect myself in the mirror and smooth out my hair before slipping out the door and toward his room, all the while formulating an excuse for if I happen to bump into anyone else on the way. Holt's room just so happens to be close to the vending machines at the end of the hall. I'm happy to blame my trip on a late-night potato chip craving.

But for the second time tonight, luck is on my side, because I don't encounter another soul until Holt pulls open his door.

"Hi," I say as his dark eyes roam over me, lingering in all his favorite places before finally settling on my face.

"You look incredible," he says, his voice low.

I'm dressed in a pair of jeans and a peach-colored T-shirt with slip-ons on my feet. I washed off all my makeup earlier, but I'm grateful for his compliment all the same.

"Thanks," I murmur, taking note of how the man fills out a pair of jeans and a T-shirt so well, it should be a crime.

I follow him into his room, which, unlike my suite, is a modest, standard hotel room. Just a mini fridge, a wingback chair in the corner, and of course, a neatly made bed. A bed that looms in the center of the room like a beacon, and at that sight, I have to remind myself to breathe.

Before I can even manage a word, Holt circles his big hands around my waist, pulling me flush against him and claiming my mouth with a firm, commanding kiss that empties the breath from my lungs.

Up until now, he's been so careful with me, toeing every line until I invite him to cross it. But not tonight. Tonight, his kiss is hot and urgent, his tongue eagerly learning every inch of mine as he fills his hands with my backside—squeezing until I release a little moan. I can feel the pressure of his erection straining against my belly through his pants, and my heart rate nearly doubles.

"Sorry. Been wanting to do that all day," he says in a low voice that makes my insides shiver with excitement.

16

HOLT

Eden looks incredible.

I haven't seen her since our little conversation in the hallway earlier, and it strikes me again just how gorgeous she really is. This time she's dressed down in jeans and a T-shirt instead of one of her usual business suits, which excites me almost as much. But there's something I like about this relaxed version of her too, the one that not many people get to see.

When she sauntered into my room tonight, I grabbed her and kissed her perfect mouth, unable to wait a second longer. My cock hardened instantly, and of course Eden noticed. Now I've put a little distance between us, getting her a bottle of water from the mini fridge just so I have something to do with my hands that has nothing to do with ripping her clothes off.

I told myself this wasn't going to happen tonight, and even though that kiss spiraled out of control fast, I'm determined not to sleep with her. Not yet, anyway.

Because if I do, I'm afraid she's going to see right through me. See that this isn't some hot game to me. See that when I touch her, it's like her skin is something to be worshipped, and her body is the most precious gift in the world. I'm afraid she'll discover all the secrets I keep hidden away. And I can't let that happen.

We sit on the bed together, and Eden takes a sip of her water before setting the bottle on the nightstand.

"Thank you for earlier," she says, her voice soft. "With Alex. I know you were protecting me."

I nod, something inside me tightening. "I'll always protect you."

My words are filled with meaning and purpose, and Eden doesn't fail to notice. Her eyes latch onto mine, and with a soft expression, she touches the back of my hand, the pads of her fingers caressing my calloused knuckles.

A simple touch shouldn't be this electrifying,

but it is. And I'm speechless.

She leans in and kisses me—just a light press of her mouth to mine at first. When my lips part, her tongue sweeps inside against mine. Then she's kissing me the way I remember from all of my best memories. Her tongue touches mine, her mouth hot and needy, tiny whimpers in the back of her throat. I grow warm all over and my cock jerks behind my zipper. It's never been this good with anyone else. Not even close.

I need to get my head on straight. She came here wanting to hook up—not to rekindle our young love.

Get a clue, Rossi. She's a woman under an enormous amount of pressure, a woman on the brink of a rebound. That's it. You're a temporary stop, just like you were before, here to lend some stress relief. Maybe an orgasm or two.

It's then that I tell myself maybe, just *maybe*, it would be okay to indulge—just for tonight. It doesn't have to mean anything. It can't.

Deciding I can live with that, I guide her back onto the bed so she's lying against the pillows and I hover over top of her. Her mouth is so perfect, and I can't get enough.

As we kiss, her hands wander. Caressing my

biceps as I support my weight over her, running over the broad planes of my chest, then down my stomach until they settle at the waistband of my jeans. I can feel her hesitate for a moment before gathering her courage, and then she palms the firm ridge of my erection through the fabric.

A low grunt pushes past my lips.

I strip her of her T-shirt and then unbutton her jeans. Eden pushes her hands under my shirt, and I slip that off too. I push her thighs together only long enough to tug her jeans down and off. Then she parts her knees again, and the sight of her lying on my bed wearing only her bra and panties, which are white and lacy, makes my breath catch. She looks good enough to eat.

I kiss her lips, her collarbone, the top of each breast, then tug down the cups of her bra so I can suck and feast on her. She moans and brings one hand to my hair, gently raking her nails along my scalp. I run my fingers over the dip in her belly until I can slip them under the elastic of her panties and touch her perfect pussy. It's so soft and warm and wet, and I groan.

"Holt . . ." She moans, her hips rocking into my hand.

I can sense she's already close, whimpering

softly as my fingers work. My cock is so hard it aches, and all the blood pumping to my groin has clouded my judgment. Continuing to caress her, I use my free hand to release my belt and open my pants. Taking myself in my hand, I stroke slowly once, needing a release so fucking badly it hurts.

Eden and I exhale a shuddering breath at the same time.

"Let me," she murmurs.

As I bend down to take her mouth, her greedy tongue matches mine stroke for stroke as she lifts her hips off the bed, pressing herself into my touch. Her hand slides up and down my shaft, and I'm sure I'm going to come too soon and ruin our good time. I force a deep breath into my lungs, fighting to get myself under control.

I can't even blame it on overactive hormones like I could back when we first shared a bed many years ago. My attraction to her has always been a powerful, dangerous thing, hell-bent on ruining everything for me. And this moment is one I've fantasized about and jacked off to countless times, as wrong as it is. Eden naked and panting, her body begging for mine . . . her kissable mouth saying my name as she comes apart.

"Holt . . ." She breathes out my name on a

moan. "I'm going to come."

"Not yet," I say, my tone commanding. I need my mouth on her first.

I kiss a path down her neck to her full breasts, which I treat to soft kisses, making my way down her body past the dip in her belly until I can settle between her thighs. Eden touches my hair as I move the fabric of her panties to the side and treat her pussy to one long, slow lick, and she makes a choked sound.

She tastes even better than I remember, and I groan low in my throat as my tongue makes greedy passes at her silken flesh.

My mouth is everywhere at once, all over her sweetness, nipping at her inner thigh with my teeth, licking her in a steady rhythm over and over as I squeeze the base of my cock to fight off my desperate need to come.

Her body quakes as she comes apart. It's a beautiful sight, and I don't let up. Her voice is rough as she climaxes, and I've never heard a more lovely or desperate sound as my name leaves her lips again.

Eden is boneless and disoriented for a moment, and I love that it was *me* who put that sleepy, satisfied look on her face. She cuddles into my arms, laying her head on my chest as her heart rate slows. As much as I love holding her, my body's insistent reminder is difficult to ignore. My cock is still hard, and frankly, a little grumpy at being ignored.

But then she seems to remember there's a steely erection pressed inconveniently between us, and she brings her hand to me again, stroking so slowly, it takes my breath away.

"Can I ask you something? Are you . . ." Her hand moves down torturously.

"Get it out, sweetheart."

"Are you sleeping with anyone?"

Shit. Now I feel like an asshole. She's trying to have a serious, adult conversation with me, and I respond with some growly, macho comment.

"Uh," is all I manage, and I'm forced to clear my throat.

"Because I was tested after Alex, and I'm cl—"

Lifting her chin, I force her gaze to mine. "I'm not sleeping with anyone. And I'm clean too. But we're not having sex tonight."

I fight back a strange wave of emotion at the thought of finally being with her in that way after all these years. She looks a little taken aback by my comment, but the truth is, I'm just not ready to go there emotionally yet with her.

"In that case, may I?" she asks sweetly, moving down the bed until she's perched between my parted thighs.

Fuck yes. Those are the words that leap into my head, but thankfully something a little more articulate comes out of my mouth.

"Anything."

She offers me a pleased smile before lowering her mouth to my groin and treating me to a slow lick. It's hot, and I love watching her. I shift, lifting onto one elbow, and move her hair from her face so I can watch her sucking on me.

Fuck.

I grunt, and Eden murmurs her approval.

"Your mouth feels so good," I say on a groan, petting her hair and tucking it behind one ear.

The sight is erotic as hell, and I lose myself in the pleasure of it. She's perfect.

The intensity of my release is unexpected. Normally, I'm quiet in bed, so I'm surprised to hear the deep groan that rumbles in my chest, and the sound of her name falling from my lips. My cock jerks in her mouth, but Eden doesn't let up, swallowing me until I'm spent and relaxed.

Finally, she releases me and sits back on her heels. "That okay?"

"Fuck." I groan again and tug her onto my chest. She laughs softly and lets me hold her. "You're incredible."

I hold her close, wondering how long she'll lie with me like this. I'm sure she's about to get up and dress and make an excuse about going back to her own room. And while I do understand that, it doesn't mean I'm happy about letting her go.

But then she sits up, pulling the sheet with her to cover her naked chest, and I can tell there's something else on her mind.

"I was wondering about something."

17

EDEN

Holt said I could ask him anything, and lying here in bed with him, I believe him. I'm sleepy and completely satisfied, and apparently that's a recipe that makes me want to reminisce. I've just asked Holt about our night together way back in college, and now he's gone quiet on me.

His chin dips and he presses a soft kiss to my forehead. "I thought it was obvious I enjoyed myself back then."

I smile in the darkness. Most of the light from outside is now gone, and there's only a soft lamp glowing dimly in the corner. "That's good. I thought about that night often over the years."

I'm not sure if I should have admitted that, but now that it's out there, I decide it's only fair—I wouldn't want to hide my truth from Holt.

"So, you never regretted it, then?" His voice is low and husky.

Surprise jolts through me. "Regret? What makes you say that?"

"You left that note," he says, his low voice a little unsteady. With each word, it sounds like he's stepping around broken glass. "I worried that I'd hurt you or something. Wondered if you felt pressured or just didn't enjoy yourself. I tried to make the right decisions, respect your boundaries and all, but that note . . . you said it was all a mistake."

He studies my palm for a moment, then releases a sigh, his sad eyes meeting mine.

"At the time, I thought it was." My voice is soft, hesitant. "I was inexperienced and so uncertain about what I wanted. Later, I realized the real mistake was running from your bed and into someone else's arms," I whisper. "But I didn't know that then. I was young and stupid."

"Hey." He sits up, leveling me with a stern look. "You've never been stupid. You graduated magna cum laude. Stupid people don't do that."

"Fair," I say, but then his words fully register, and the slightest smile tugs at my lips. "But wait.

How did you know I graduated magna cum laude? Did you check on me after you left Sutton?"

He lifts a shoulder, and if I'm not mistaken, the faintest flush appears on the apples of his cheeks. "Can't blame me for being curious about the gorgeous, mysterious girl who came into my life for one perfect night and then disappeared for good."

"Not for good, it turns out," I murmur, nuzzling into his chest.

It's a little dangerous to be this vulnerable with him, I admit. I have no idea where a man like Holt fits into my life. What I do know, however, is that being with him in this moment feels right, logistics aside. So I snuggle in a little tighter, enjoying the feel of his heartbeat on my cheek. But when I feel myself start to doze off, I know it's time to go.

"It's late," I say through a yawn. "I'd better get back to my room."

He sighs. "I wish you wouldn't."

"I wish that too. But it's for the best."

Reluctantly, I peel myself away from him, immediately missing his touch the moment it's gone. I collect my clothes from the end of the bed, and Holt does the same with his boxers, hiking them up over his hips before tugging on a pair of sweats from his suitcase. At the door, he treats me to another long, slow kiss, the kind that makes me wish I could say *fuck it* and crawl back into his bed for the night.

There's nothing I'd love more than to spend the rest of the evening wrapped in his arms. But there's also nothing that would ruin my career quicker. So with one last squeeze of his hand, I slip out the door.

"Good night, Holt," I whisper.

He smiles back. "Sweet dreams."

But we both know *sweet* won't even begin to describe what I'll be dreaming of.

18

EDEN

"I think I'm going to freeze to death."

Gretchen pulls together the sides of her thick cardigan, frowning at me from across the wrought-iron table. When I invited her to have lunch with me this afternoon, I may have omitted the detail that I reserved a table on the patio, and she hasn't stopped shivering from the moment we sat down.

"You're being dramatic," I tease, grabbing my phone and swiping open the weather app for evidence. "See? Fifty-six degrees. It's practically summer."

Okay, maybe I'm exaggerating, but so is she. Besides, with all the traveling I've been doing lately, I haven't gotten the chance to enjoy my favorite season in my favorite city. From our table at this

Back Bay brunch spot, we have a stellar view of the Public Garden, where all the trees are blazing with bright yellows and deep reds. Fall in Boston is not to be missed.

"Maybe this is considered summer in Antarctica," Gretchen grumbles, warming up with a big sip of her chai tea. "Remind me why I haven't moved to Bora Bora yet?"

"Because there probably aren't a lot of tax accountant positions open in the tropics," I remind her. "And you'd miss me too much. Based on how much you've been texting me during away games, I think you might actually explode if we were permanently located in different time zones."

The mention of my travel schedule quickly takes her mind off the cold. Her eyes light up as she leans forward with both forearms planted on the table. "Yeah, Little Miss New Zip Code Every Weekend. How has everything been going?"

"Pretty well." I sip my oat-milk latte, dusting off the Titans scores I keep filed in the back of my mind. "We lost four to three against Detroit, but Cleveland was a huge victory, five to one. So fingers crossed for Toronto tonight. It's sort of weird not being with the team this weekend, but it is nice to have some time off."

Gretchen's frown is back and deeper than ever. "I read the hockey blogs, Eden. I know the scores. What I want to know is what *your* scorecard looks like with you-know-who." She grins at me expectantly.

We're interrupted by our waitress, delivering Gretchen's panini and my broccoli-and-cheddar soup. While my best friend picks the tomatoes out of her sandwich, I have a moment to choose my words. I knew this conversation was coming, but I didn't exactly plan a script.

"You're not getting out of that question," Gretchen says, pointing a sweet potato fry at me. "What happened with you and Holt?"

"A few things happened," I say slowly, dragging my spoon through my bowl and scooping up a heaping portion of soup. It's warm and luxurious on my tongue, but more importantly, it buys me a few more precious moments before having to tell my best friend how wrong her advice was. "Turns out, your idea to *get him out of my system* wasn't exactly effective."

She arches a brow at me, urging me to continue. "Go on."

"Well, against my better judgment, we hooked up twice," I say, my focus more on my soup than on her. "Not sex, but you know . . ." My voice drops to a quiet murmur. "Other stuff."

"And?" she asks. "How did said *other stuff* go?"

I sigh, looking down at the table between us. "All it did was make me want him more."

I'm expecting another frown in response, but when I glance at Gretchen, her lips are curled in a devious, self-satisfied smirk, like a supervillain hatching a plan. "I sort of had a feeling it would."

"What?" My voice errs on the side of too loud for a public conversation, but I'm too shocked to correct my volume. "Then why did you tell me it would get him out of my system?"

She lifts a shoulder, a wicked gleam dancing through her green eyes. "Because he's hot, and you wouldn't have done it otherwise."

A laugh of disbelief threatens to sneak past my lips. "You're crazy, you know that?"

"No, you're crazy," she says insistently. "You're the one who made us sit outside in the cold today. I'm just being a good friend and making sure you get laid."

This time, there's no restraining my laughter.

I can't believe Gretchen, but with how absolutely incredible things with Holt have been, I probably should be thanking her. That is, as long as no one finds out about us. Otherwise, all this giddy excitement would blow up in my face and make everything about my position so much harder. I think the team is actually starting to respect me now.

After I've had a few more spoonfuls of soup, my phone vibrates with a calendar reminder. One hour until I need to be at the arena. I swipe out of the notification, wave down the waitress, and ask for the check.

"Are you leaving?" Gretchen asks, disappointed. "You haven't even gotten to the juicy parts."

"We're hosting a kids' clinic at the arena today," I say. "I have to be there early to give the opening remarks to a bunch of mini hockey legends in the making."

"Can't the mini hockey legends wait a little bit longer?" She juts out her lower lip as far as it goes. "You can't withhold details from me now."

"I can and I will," I say, grinning as I scribble my signature across the bottom of the check and slip my credit card back into my wallet. Gretchen's puppy-dog eyes don't have power over me anymore, and even if they did, they can't compete with work obligations.

"Why don't you just get Aspen to do it? The kids won't know the difference between the team owner and the team owner's assistant," Gretchen points out.

I roll my eyes. "Sure, and then I'll just have Aspen run the whole team too, on top of managing my entire professional life." Even if Aspen is amazing at her job, that would hardly be fair. I'm already conscious of how many hours she's working—and it's a lot.

"Technically, that would make *her* Holt's employer, right? Not you? Maybe then you could bang him without any guilt." Gretchen's eyebrows jump up and down suggestively, but I shoot her a stern look and she stops. "Sorry, sorry," she grumbles, waving me off. "I'll take care of the tip. Tell the kiddos I said hi."

"Thanks, Gretch. Gotta run." I smile, tossing in a wave as I exit the patio.

It's a ten-minute walk back to my condo, just long enough for me to pop in my earbuds and listen to the first three songs on the playlist Holt shared with me. The gritty vocals and atmospheric guitar solos send adrenaline pulsing through my veins. He was right. This is the perfect pump-up music for any situation.

By the time I make it home, I have forty-five minutes until I have to be at the arena, just long enough to put the finishing touches on my speech. A few run-throughs in my bathroom mirror later, I'm feeling confident and ready.

Maybe the playlist wasn't the only thing Holt was right about.

As I rehearse the lines I wrote about believing in yourself and working as a team, I realize my words perfectly reflect what he said to me the other night. A team is more than just one player or one coach. It's a living, breathing organism made up of different essential parts, and if I take on the pressure of the entire Titans organization, I'm going to crumple. I have to trust others to do their part, and focus on what's in front of me.

And today, that's giving a speech to a bunch of eager ten-year-olds on skates.

I've got this. I'm a Wynn, and Wynns don't fail. Always Wynn, no matter what.

I repeat the family mantra in my head as I slip into a pair of black booties and my camel-colored topcoat, giving the jeans and sweater I wore to lunch a bit of a professional edge. Not that these kids would mind if I showed up in an oversized hockey jersey, but this outfit makes me look as un-stoppable as I feel right now.

While I'm applying a fresh coat of lipstick, my phone buzzes with another calendar reminder. Only twenty minutes until speech time. *Time to hustle.* Luckily, there's barely a heel on these boo-ties, and I'm in the parking garage and slipping into my SUV in no time, rehearsing my speech in my head as I back out of the garage.

"Ever since I was a little girl, hockey has been an important part of my—"

Crunch.

My stomach lurches back against my spine at the sound of metal crashing against metal.

Oh God, no. Not right now. This can't be hap-pening.

I squeeze my eyes shut, sucking in a breath through gritted teeth. But I can't hide from what I've done forever, so I pry one eye open, then the other, turning cautiously to peek over one shoulder to assess the damage.

Shit. I hit the freaking garage door. Way to go, Eden.

A string of curse words pile up in my throat as I climb out of my car to inspect the damage on the garage door. I've seen worse, but I've also sure as hell seen better. When I click the button on the fob provided by the condo building to open the door, there's a harsh gear-grinding sound, but no movement.

Looks like my SUV isn't going anywhere, and neither am I. So much for my speech to the next generation of Titans.

My stomach churns with a nauseating combination of frustration and anger, mixed with a heavy dose of self-doubt. Just when I was starting to feel confident in my role, I go and do something completely stupid. I can't even back out of my own parking garage without screwing it up, and I'm supposed to be in charge of a pro hockey team?

As always, I do the only thing I know how to do in times like these. I pace. And then I pull my phone from my coat pocket and call the first person who comes to mind.

"Hello?"

Just the sound of Holt's low, gravelly voice on the other end of the line brings my panic down from a ten to a seven.

"I need your help," I whisper, chewing anxiously at my lip as I begin my explanation about my car being stuck, but before I can say another word, he speaks.

"I'll be there as soon as I can." His voice is cool and calm, providing instant relief to my tightly wound system.

Either he was nearby, or he has no regard for speed limits, because hardly five minutes pass before Holt ducks under the partially open door of the garage. I'm leaning against the cold concrete wall, chomping on a hangnail, when he slips an arm around my waist, pressing a kiss into my hair.

"Accident, huh?"

I nod, trying to wrestle back the tears welling up in my eyes. I don't know if I'm crying because of the car, or the fact that he was so quick to rush to my rescue. But either way, he wipes my tears with his thumbs, then pulls me against his chest, smoothing my hair with his palm.

"It's going to be okay, Eden. It's just a little accident. Everyone is entitled to a few mistakes now and then."

The tears are coming steadily now, which makes me feel like even more of an idiot. It's just a little mistake, but it's the last thing I needed right now.

"I feel so stupid," I manage to choke out

through sniffles.

He pulls me in again, letting me break down for just a moment in his arms. But I guess Holt Rossi is accepting no pity parties today, because as soon as my breaths slow down, he unhooks his keys from his belt loop, unfurling my fist to place them in my palm.

"Don't feel stupid. It could have happened to anyone. Breathe, Eden. This is no big deal. We'll get it fixed, okay?"

I nod, starting to believe him. "I'm supposed to be giving a speech for the kids' clinic at the arena in . . ." I check my watch, drawing a big breath. "Fifteen minutes."

"My car's outside. Take it."

My brow creases and my tears subside. "But then how will you—"

He shakes his head adamantly. "Nope. No arguing. Just do it. You've got kids waiting for you, and I know a repairman I can call. Give me your keys. I'll wait here while it gets handled."

Reluctant, I place my key ring in his big palm. "Are you sure about this?"

He gives me a firm nod, wiping the last of my tears away. "Now go inspire the hell out of those kids."

"Th-thank you," I sputter, a hint of a smile pulling at my lips. "I really can't thank you enough for all of—"

Before I can finish the thought, he cuts me off with a firm, silencing kiss that warms every inch of my body. "Go wow 'em, sweetheart," he whispers, giving my shoulder a reassuring squeeze.

"Okay," I whisper back, then hurry out to his car, wondering how and why he seems to know just the right things to say to make everything seem okay.

• • •

The second I step out of the arena, I dig my phone from my pocket and dial Holt.

He picks up on the first ring. "Hey, how'd it go?"

"So well." I sigh, sandwiching my phone between my ear and my shoulder as I fish his car keys from my purse. "The kids were super-sweet and attentive. I'd love to tell you about it over dinner, if you don't have plans."

This man was my own personal superhero today. The least I can do is feed him.

"Dinner sounds great."

I can hear his smile through the phone, and I smile back, knowing I'll get to see him in just a few minutes. "Perfect. I'll order something for delivery. Chinese sound okay?"

We agree on two orders of kung pao chicken, fried rice, and egg rolls, and he waits on the line while I tap our order into an app.

"The site says it'll be there in twenty. Meet you in the lobby?"

"Done and done," he says. "See you soon."

If I were driving my own car, I'd probably speed the whole way home with how eager I am to see him, but since I've already been in one fender bender today, I hug the right lane the whole way back to my condo.

When I pull up to the parking garage, I'm surprised to see that the garage door is already fixed and fully operational, and when I drive past my own car, the dent on the back bumper is less severe than I remember. Not saying that the car accident was a good thing, but between the minimal damage and the very sexy dinner date I've secured as a result of the ordeal, I feel as though things have balanced out nicely.

When I enter my building, Holt's imposing figure makes him easy to spot right away. While the other residents filter in and out of the elevators, he stands in the very center of the lobby, a slight grin on his mouth and a plastic bag full of small white takeout boxes dangling from his fingers.

He greets me by pressing a quick kiss against my cheekbone. Instantly, my temperature shoots up several degrees. He's never kissed me in public before, and even if it's just on the cheek, I'm amazed by how special it makes me feel.

Maybe my instincts should have prompted me to scan the lobby for onlookers or, worse yet, a camera-happy blogger ready to report on any newsworthy move I might make. But none of that crosses my mind until we're unpacking our dinner on my kitchen island, and by then, it's too late anyway. Being with Holt makes all my worry subside. He's magical that way.

"I can't believe the garage door is already fixed," I say as I press onto my tiptoes, grabbing two square white plates from my cabinet. This dinner isn't the fanciest thank-you in the world, so the least I can do is serve it on real plates.

"I told you, I know a repairman," Holt says.

"He's good."

"If he got that whole project done in under two hours, he's not just good. He's superhuman. I really can't thank you enough."

"This is as good of a thank-you as a man could ever want." Holt smiles, jutting a thumb toward the takeout boxes.

"Do you want to watch the game while we eat? Puck drop is in ten."

"Sure," he says. "Let's do it."

I'm usually too much of a neat freak to eat such messy food anywhere other than the table, but nothing in the world sounds better than cozying up on the couch with Holt, dinner, and a game we're predicted to win.

With full plates, we assume the same spots on the couch as the last time Holt was here, the night of the big team dinner. But unlike that night, there's no awkwardness, no readjusting to each other. Instead, we sit close enough that my thigh presses against his, and he listens attentively as I recount my afternoon with the best and brightest young hockey players in Boston.

"I swear, some of these ten-year-olds can skate as well as our players," I say with a laugh.

"You'll be drafting those same kids in ten years," he points out. "Just you wait."

As I'm turning that thought over, Holt slips his fingers between mine. His palm is warm and rough with calluses, and my heart rate quickens as he runs his thumb along the back of my hand.

I told Gretchen (and myself) that all I wanted was some hot, sweaty fun. So, why are my emotions all over the freaking place right now? Because of the history Holt and I share? That deep, brief connection that ended so quickly?

I take a moment, trying to breathe deeply and calm down before I embarrass myself with a display of emotion that has no place in a casual relationship like this one.

Get it together, Eden. Maybe I'm just feeling grateful that he saved me earlier in my jam . . . that has to be it.

"I'm proud of you for bouncing back so quickly after your accident," Holt says, unaware of my inner dialogue. "I'll bet your speech made those kids' whole year."

"I couldn't have done it without you," I say truthfully, blinking up at him with an appreciative smile. "And not just because you let me borrow your car. The things you said to me the other night about working as a team and just handling my own role? It really helped me."

"Yeah?" His full lips tick upward. "I'm happy to help you with anything you need."

Just the suggestion sends heat flooding through my system. "You sure?" I whisper, wetting my lower lip with a sweep of my tongue. "Because there's something pretty important I need your help with right now."

"Yeah? Anything for you."

My free hand floats to the stubble on his cheek, taking him in—chiseled jaw, gray eyes, and velvety lips. "I need you to kiss me right now."

"I think I can take care of that." His head tilts, and his warm, eager lips meet mine in a slow, sweet kiss that prompts every hair on my arms to stand on end.

One gentle kiss becomes two, and when he touches his tongue against my lips, they part, welcoming him in. Soon, his big hands are in my hair, pulling me close to him as our tongues intertwine in an easy dance that only we know the steps to. When he breaks away, I lean in again, capturing his mouth with mine. Nothing could pull me away from him right now.

"Eden, honey. Knock-knock."

Well, allow me to immediately take that back. There's one thing—one person, rather—who could make me leap a full foot away from this man, and she just waltzed through the door.

"M—Mom?" I stutter, jumping to my feet and quickly finger-combing my hair. "What the h— heck are you doing here?"

Holt's eyes widen as he silently mouths a question. *Did you know she was coming?*

I shake my head, then plaster on a smile as my mother's heels click around the corner. Her brows shoot up and she presses a hand to her chest when she sees I'm not alone.

"Oh, I beg your pardon. Didn't the front desk notify you that I was coming up?"

"My phone is still in my purse," I say, instantly regretting that choice. Unless I'm working, I don't really text anyone other than Gretchen and Holt these days. I didn't even think to grab it.

"That's very concerning," she murmurs through pursed lips. "Anyone could wander in here off the streets." She quickly appraises Holt, then turns her thin-lipped frown back to me.

"I promise, I've never had a security issue," I

tell her, biting back the *until now* that I'd like to tack onto that statement. I love my mother, I really do, but now is not the time for a surprise visit.

"I heard you weren't traveling with the team tonight and thought I'd swing by to say hello. I didn't realize you already had company."

Well, I guess we're doing introductions now. Love that for me.

"This is Holt Rossi. He's head of the security firm we hired on for the Titans this year." I gesture to Holt and he shoves up from the couch, clearing his throat before extending a hand to her.

"It's a pleasure to meet you, Ms. Wynn."

She places her hand in his, confusion written all over her small features. "I go by Baker now." And then the crease in her brow deepens. "I hadn't heard about additional security."

"Just an extra precaution for Eden," Holt says gruffly, then shifts his gaze back to me. "I should get going. Glad we could talk through those security guidelines, ma'am."

I offer him a sad smile. As grateful as I am that he's sparing us any further awkwardness by playing it professional, a pang of guilt twinges in my chest that he feels like he has to lie about why he's here. "Thanks for everything, Holt."

"Have a great evening," my mother says, her tone sweet and genuine. But before Holt can leave, she turns back to me with a sharp frown. "Eden, honey, I thought you took the weekend off. Why are you bringing work home with you? You need time off. Maybe you need a date."

Little does she know that she just interrupted one.

19

HOLT

When my phone chimes with another text, I assume it's Madden again. He and I have been going back and forth about this week's schedule, in addition to him giving me a relentless ribbing over his perceived crush I have on Eden. Little does he know how true his words were, though I played it off well.

But when I check the screen, it's not a text from Madden. It's Eden. I made it home from her place a little while ago so she could visit with her mom. Her text is a welcome distraction from work.

I park my ass on the stool in the kitchen and read her note. I'm so sorry about my mom.

That's okay, I write back.

Little bubbles bounce on my screen for a few seconds. I know she can be a bit much.

I type out my reply with a smirk on my lips. Maybe she was right. Maybe you do need a date.

Ha-ha, she writes. Then she adds a laughing-face emoji.

Alone in my kitchen, I chuckle and take another sip from the bottle of water sitting beside me. Another text comes through from Madden, but I ignore it. Then I dial Eden's number, and she answers on the first ring.

"Hey." She sounds slightly breathless, or maybe just surprised that I called instead of replying to her text. But I'm not really a texting kind of guy.

"I'm serious. About that date. Could I take you out sometime?"

She's quiet for a second, and I wonder what she's thinking. "We've never had one of those."

"I know. I thought it might be time."

My voice is steady, but inside, I feel less certain. And for a second, a flash of insecurity hits me and doubt creeps in.

Maybe she doesn't want to go out with you. Maybe you're better off being her dirty little secret. Maybe she doesn't want to be seen with you in public.

But when she speaks again, I can tell she's smiling. "I'm free tomorrow."

I smile too. "Perfect. It's a date. Would six work?"

Eden chuckles. "Yes. What did you have in mind?"

I run a hand through my hair, still grinning. *God, this is fun.* "It's a surprise, but I promise it won't involve hockey or shellfish."

She laughs. "Okay, that sounds perfect."

• • •

I spend the entire next day cleaning my apartment because it's rare that I have visitors. Since I thought Eden might like something more low-key, I invited her over to my place tonight and told her I'd cook for her. A chill night in sounded like a good idea at the time, but now I'm second-guessing myself.

Surveying my work, I let out a sigh. It's not as nice as Eden's condo, but that doesn't mean I'm going to be self-conscious about it.

My apartment is a small one-bedroom in a good location, and the fact that the kitchen isn't outfitted with sleek stainless steel or all the latest gadgets doesn't bother me. I have what I need and not a thing more. Plus, I have a kick-ass balcony that I've decorated with cushions and white-string lights and warm flannel blankets, where I pictured us cuddled together under the stars as I cleaned today.

God, I sound like a sap, and I don't even care.

My sheets have been washed, just in case things progress to the bedroom, and I even made sure to squeeze in some manscaping. So basically, I'm one thousand percent ready for this date tonight.

My phone rings, and for a second I think it might be Eden. Maybe something came up at the last minute. Maybe she needs to cancel. I sure as hell hope not.

But when I check the screen, it's not Eden's name I see. It's my mom's. My stomach sinks as I stab the ANSWER button with my thumb.

"Hello?" There's irritation in my voice, but it's nothing compared to the frustration I feel at the next words out of my mother's mouth.

20

EDEN

I park outside Holt's building at exactly six o'clock with a smile on my lips. I've never been here before, but I've been almost giddy with excitement all day.

First, I spent a ridiculous amount of time getting ready, even though he promised it was a very casual date at his place. After a lengthy shower, where I made sure to shave all the important parts, I blew out my hair and did my makeup with care.

Now I'm dressed in a pair of slim-fit dark jeans, and since the fall air is cool enough to warrant it, my favorite deep V-neck sweater in creamy oatmeal with what I'm hoping will be my secret weapon underneath—a push-up bra and matching panties in black satin. I can only imagine Holt's expression when he discovers them.

With a deep breath, I head up the stairs to the apartment Holt indicated in his last text. I'm filled with anticipation. Maybe it's because aside from Alex, I haven't dated much. Or maybe I had such a surprisingly good time with Holt on the road, I'm eager for more time with the man I can't stop thinking about.

I find his unit at the end of the hall and pause at his door to knock, my lips already twitching with the hint of a smile. After waiting about a minute with no answer, I press my ear to the door. It's quiet inside, no voices or sounds of music, so I knock again.

As I wait, my smile starts to fade.

Still nothing.

I twist the doorknob, and finding it unlocked, peek my head inside. "Holt?" I call as I step through the doorway.

His place is compact, but clean and organized. It suits him. Nothing is out of place, and I can picture him here, rifling through the mail on the counter after work, or doing some push-ups in the center of the living room floor.

After a quick glance around the living room with its large gray couch and flatscreen TV, I spot him on the balcony outside, just beyond the glass doors at the end of the living room. He's facing away from me, his hands gripping the railing and his head tipped down as though he's studying his feet.

My good mood from moments ago is gone. Seeing him looking distressed like this brings a whole new set of emotions crashing through me—and a whole lot of confusion.

Suddenly Holt turns, and when he registers me here, standing in his living room, a look of uncertainty crosses his features. His posture is stiff, his shoulders set back as he stalks toward me. There's something in his eyes I've never seen before. An empty, haunted look. I feel like I've done something wrong, but I have no idea what. It's disorienting.

I swallow past the nerves in my throat, wondering what's happened. What's brought about this change in him. But I can do nothing but wait, because Holt doesn't seem in a hurry to fill me in.

I shouldn't be here. That's the first thought that flits through my brain.

My heart pounds out a heavy rhythm as he comes closer, stopping beside the sofa where I stand. He lets out a heavy sigh and fists his hands at his sides.

"Is everything okay?"

With a curt nod, he continues appraising me coolly, but he offers nothing else. A wealth of emotions are hidden in his gaze, but I couldn't begin to tell you what he's feeling. Mostly there's a vacant look that makes my stomach tighten.

"Because I feel like something's wrong," I say.

He gives his head a cursory shake. "It's fine."

I don't feel *fine*. I feel like I could cry, and I don't even know *why*. If everything's going to fall apart around me, I'd at least want to know the reason why. I deserve that much.

But he won't even look at me, and a shiver creeps over my skin. I wrap my arms around myself, preparing for the worst. Holt stays silent, though, so I have no clue where his head is at.

Beyond him, I peer out at the balcony, with two inviting lounge chairs, complete with plush cushions and sherpa-lined flannel blankets. Flickering candles and a string of white twinkle lights complete the look. It's romantic as all get-out, but the effort of it doesn't match with the stony-faced man I see standing before me.

"Well, I . . ." I pause, clearing my throat. "If something's come up, or now is a bad time, I can just—"

"It's fine," he mutters again, but he doesn't meet my gaze.

It stings more than I care to admit. Tears blur my eyes, but I refuse to cry.

Where is the man who swept me into his arms and kissed me senseless the moment I entered his hotel room? Where is the man I cuddled with after our steamy session in that hotel bed? I sensed he didn't want to let me go that night, and now it's the complete opposite . . . it's like he doesn't want me here. I have no idea what could have possibly changed since he invited me over last night.

"I'm sorry. I don't know if you've changed your mind, or . . ." I take a step back, and he doesn't try to stop me. "I think I'll just go," I manage to say, my voice a little shaky.

Even as I say the words, he looks detached, his eyes looking anywhere but directly at me.

A hot flood of anger and rejection rage inside me. *What a dick. Why couldn't he just be honest and tell me he isn't interested?*

I suddenly feel so foolish for my wide-eyed optimism about how tonight would unfold. I blow-dried my hair. Wore my best lingerie. But fuck this.

I'm not going to beg for any man's attention. I have more self-respect than that.

With purposeful strides, I head for the door, but three steps in and Holt catches me around the waist.

"Eden."

My name on his lips is rough, almost broken. It guts me.

I turn to face him. "What?"

"I'm sorry." He exhales slowly, looking pained. "Let me explain."

"What happened?" I hate the broken sound of my voice, but I'm near tears and barely holding it together.

"My mom called. Just before you came."

I hear his words, but they make no sense. I don't understand what one thing has to do with the other. "Okay." When he doesn't say anything else, I begin to soften. "Is everything okay?"

He runs one hand over the day-old stubble on his jaw. "Yes and no. Do you want to sit down?"

I hesitate, and then decide I'm being a terrible guest. Clearly, something is wrong to make Holt react this way. Deciding to show him compassion, even when I feel the need to guard my heart, I gesture to the sofa. "Let's sit."

He follows me to the couch and takes the seat beside me. With a heavy exhale, Holt looks down at the floor. "I'm sorry I ruined our date."

He looks like a man who has a lot on his mind, and my heart goes out to him. "Will you tell me the reason a therapist gave you that book?"

He looks somewhat surprised by my question, but he turns to me and meets my eyes. "We're similar in that we take on too much. I don't own a hockey franchise, but at that time, when I went to the therapist, I had the weight of the world on my shoulders in other ways. Decided it might help if I talked to someone."

I take his big rough hand and squeeze. "You can tell me, Holt."

He clears his throat and shifts uncomfortably. "My mom is an addict. She's been addicted to pain pills for as long as I can remember."

It's the last thing in the world I expected him to say. I recall him telling me about his shaky family connections, but he never mentioned drug use. I sensed that they just weren't all that close. I never suspected trauma, and it makes me ache for him. It also makes me understand him a bit more, why he's so guarded. He's no doubt been through some hard times.

"A few years ago, I got so burned out and tired and depressed from always having to be the one to take care of her. Picking up the pieces for the thousandth time without knowing if anything can ever be fixed is mentally exhausting."

I nod reassuringly and wait for him to continue.

"I decided to go and talk to someone. She made me see that I play one small role, being a good son, but beyond that—my mom's sobriety, the costs for rehab—all of it wasn't my responsibility."

"It sounds like it was good advice."

He nods. "Yeah. I guess."

"So, what happened tonight? Is she okay?"

With a sorrowful look, he meets my gaze. "She's been in and out of rehab many times. Tonight she had a relapse."

"Is she okay?" I hear myself asking.

He nods. "For now. Yes, I guess so." With a heavy sigh, he puts his head in his hands. "It's just such a mess."

I press a hand to his shoulder and rub, not knowing what else to do.

A moment later, he opens his eyes and looks over at me. "Thanks. I'm sorry about all of this."

Shaking my head, I correct him. "You have nothing to be sorry for."

My emotions are all over the place. First, there's a flooding sense of relief that he hasn't rejected me, but it's short-lived because his mother's situation sounds grim. I listen as he fills me in on his childhood, on what it was like growing up with a mom addicted to drugs, and he holds little back.

After a while, I wrap Holt in a big hug, which he returns. We stay like that for a few minutes, and when we pull back, I feel calmer. I hope he does too.

We decide to pour some wine and order a pizza because the meal he planned to make tonight has been long forgotten. And I am more than okay with that, because . . . *pizza*. And *Holt*. It's a win-win.

We refill our wineglasses and take our slices on paper plates out to the balcony that looks so inviting. And it is. As we settle under blankets, little lights twinkle around us.

Our conversations tonight have turned deeper, and even though I feel for him, I actually love that he's sharing part of himself with me.

And it's far from one-sided. I share memories from my childhood too. About my dad's run for office, and my parents' later divorce. *Ugh. That was rough.* As was my breakup with Alex, which we touch on briefly.

But then Holt changes the subject, and I'm grateful. I sense he doesn't want to hear all the gory details any more than I want to relive them. It's in the past. With a pang of emotion, I wish Holt's troubles were in the rearview mirror too. I have no idea what's going to happen with his mom, but I can see by the set of his shoulders it's something that weighs heavily on him.

We finish our food but linger together, huddled under the warmth of a blanket.

"Thanks for opening up to me tonight. I want you to know, you don't have to hide those things from me."

He gives me a grim smile. "You mean the ugly parts."

I shake my head and press a hand to his cheek. "There's nothing ugly about you, Holt Rossi."

My words are the absolute truth. He's courageous and beautiful. And kind and protective. The depth of my feelings for him scare me. I still don't know where we stand, and I have no idea why, but everything seems like it could be on the verge of crumbling. Only I hope that's not the case.

He glances to the street below before meeting my gaze. "Did you ever want something you can't have?"

A wave of lust rolls through me. "Yes." My voice is just a whisper.

21

HOLT

I guide Eden to my bedroom as my heart pounds steadily.

Part of me can't believe this is happening. I thought I ruined our date earlier with my foul mood, but Eden doesn't look bothered by any of that. She climbs onto the bed and dutifully lifts her arms so I can remove her sweater.

Dressed in a black bra and dark jeans, she looks like a sexy temptress. I have no idea how I've ended up lucky enough to get her into bed tonight.

As we kiss, Eden unsnaps her bra, momentarily distracting me. She's so damn beautiful. I caress her breasts while her hand drifts south, causing a stir of arousal in my boxers.

Between kisses, we take turns removing each

other's clothes. Eden isn't the shy, uncertain girl she once was. She wants this—wants *me*. That much is obvious by the way she tugs at my belt to free it from my jeans. My body hums with anticipation.

After several minutes of removing and tossing stray articles of clothing to the floor, we lie together bare, kissing and moving as her breathy sighs and soft moans succeed at cranking my libido to an uncomfortable twelve out of ten.

She kisses me like this moment is important, like I mean something to her other than being a guy she can swap a few orgasms with. It's a dangerous thought for me to be thinking because I know the gulf that separates us.

Forcing myself to break the kiss, I move to my side and grab a condom from the nightstand. *Keep a clear head, Rossi.* This isn't important or special. It's just a hookup. Just like the one we shared in college that wasn't even meaningful enough for Eden to stick around for until morning.

"Let me help with that," she murmurs, taking the condom from me and working it down onto my shaft.

I've never had a woman help with this task, but something about her touch makes it all the more erotic. I hover over her and plant gentle kisses on her throat as I line myself up between her parted thighs. She keeps her eyes on mine as I slowly press forward, beginning to ease myself inside.

My eyes sink closed as pleasure sizzles through my body. She's so damn warm and wet, and every inch of her is inviting. It's an almost spiritual moment.

I keep my pace slow, leisurely at first. I can't ruin this by coming yet, as much as my body is in favor of that idea. The base of my spine tingles and my balls ache. But I have to make this equally as good for Eden.

I want to confess so many things to her, but the words catch in my throat. I want to promise to always keep her safe. I want to beg her to stay with me—always. I want her to be mine and no one else's.

Of course, I say none of those things out loud because I learned a long time ago that hope is a dangerous thing. Eden will probably get her fill of me and move on once she realizes where we each are in the pecking order.

I chase the sad thought away with a steady snapping of my hips. She whimpers, pressing her pelvis to mine, meeting me stroke for stroke.

"Fuck, you feel good," I say, groaning.

"So do you." She sounds breathless, and I love it. Love knowing that I'm driving her wild with desire, just like she does to me.

"Did you ever think about it?" she asks, surprising me.

"This?" I breathe out the word, pressing my mouth to her throat, and she nods. "All the time. Did you?"

I'm dying to hear her answer. Did she think about us fucking as often as I did?

Eden meets my eyes, and like she's admitting to a long-guarded secret, she nods.

Male pride surges through me, and my pulse rate increases. So does my tempo.

We've waited so long for this moment, and now that it's here, it's even better than I could have anticipated. I feel . . . well, pleasure, obviously, but there's also a sense of peace I didn't expect. We're like two halves of a whole, finally together again. No one understands me quite the way Eden seems to.

"Holt," she cries, pressing her fingernails into my shoulder. "There."

It's better than I imagined it would be when she starts to come. And believe me, I imagined it a lot—what our first time together might feel like. It's so intense, I don't know how I'll ever recover.

My release tears through me, dismantling me from the inside out. A hot rush of pleasure that rips the air from my lungs and makes my body jerk once, twice. *Fuck.*

When I untangle us and peer down at Eden, she's smiling. "What?"

She tips her chin, playing coy. But in my head, I pretend that she's thinking, *If I'd known you were so good at that, I wouldn't have waited six years.*

And hell, maybe it's true.

22

HOLT

"You didn't have to do all this, you know." Eden gives me a shy look from across the center console of my car.

Yes, I did. I ruined what was supposed to be our last date. After I got a panicked phone call from my mom, my mood had plummeted and I didn't have the energy to cook for Eden like I promised. While we ended up more than salvaging the date, ordering takeout and cuddling . . . and then, well, things turned physical and I have zero complaints there.

But it wasn't the same as having a nice date. And I didn't want to leave her hanging. Eden is the kind of woman who deserves to be wined and dined.

Then why exactly am I taking her on a date to a

drive-in movie theater, you ask?

Maybe because I know most guys would plan something extravagant to try to impress the wealthy heiress. I also know she couldn't care less about pomp and circumstance. I'm hoping she enjoys this casual downtime together.

I reach over and grab her hand, giving her a smile. "I didn't have to. But I wanted to."

She smiles, settling in beside me as I pull into the drive-in's gravel parking lot for our evening of a double feature. Since she likes nineties music, I guessed that she'd like nineties movies too, and the theater is showing some classics—first *Legally Blonde*, followed by *Scream*.

Eden's eyes widen as she takes in our surroundings. It's a weekday night, so there are only a handful of other cars here, all spaced out to give everyone plenty of breathing room.

"Have you ever been here before?"

She shakes her head. "No. Isn't that crazy? This place has been here for like forty years."

I nod. "It has. I only came once before. I think you'll like it."

I back into a parking space and open the tailgate of my SUV to let the cool evening breeze in and give us a clear view of the movie screen beyond.

"Shall we?" I ask, gesturing to the back. I've laid down the rear seats and padded the cargo area with blankets and pillows.

With a giggle, Eden climbs to the back. "This is awesome." She sighs, snuggling into the warm fleece blankets.

Thankfully, it's not too chilly tonight, but it's cool enough that we'll have to cuddle up to stay warm. *Perfect*.

I join her in the back and pop open the small cooler I've stowed beneath the seats. "Rosé?"

She grins and holds out both hands. "Yes. Please."

I chuckle and pour her a glass in a disposable cup. Eden accepts the cup and takes a small sip of the chilled wine while I set out the snacks I've packed—chocolate-covered peanuts, white cheddar popcorn, and bags of miniature pretzels.

"There's snacks too?" she asks excitedly.

"Plenty of snacks. And if we get hungrier than this, there's a hot dog stand over there. I'll go pillage for us."

She chuckles. "The perfect man."

The compliment radiates a contented warmth through me. While it's far from true, I decide to bask in that emotion for a moment longer.

It's still light outside, but the sun has started to set, casting everything with a pretty pink glow. The screen lights up with movie previews, and I adjust the volume on my car stereo so we can listen. Eden has a dreamy sort of smile on her face as we recline on the makeshift bed of pillows in the back of my SUV.

"This has got to be the best date in the history of dates." She gives me a soft, appreciative look. "Thank you for planning this. It's exactly what I needed to relax."

I nod. She's been under a lot of pressure as a team owner, and while the Titans have had a good start to their season, it's far from over. "You deserve a night off."

I lean down and press a kiss to her forehead. I'm sure most guys who had the chance to take *the* Eden Wynn out on a date would have gone much more high-end than six-dollar movie tickets and a bagful of snacks from the gas station. But I'm really fucking happy she's pleased.

"Thanks for this, Holt. It reminds me of something I'd do in high school. A date at the drive-in. Except it's better than high school, because I don't have to be nervous about whether you're going to try to get in my pants later."

I chuckle and gaze down at her. "Believe me, I'm going to try."

She laughs and playfully swats my thigh. "You can try, but just know I'm here for this movie. I haven't seen vintage Reese Witherspoon in years. And pass me some of that popcorn, would you?"

I obey, handing her a bag of popcorn and refilling her wine.

Our time together is effortless and easy, and isn't something I take for granted. While it's true I haven't dated much, there were a few women in between first hooking up with Eden and now. None of them made me feel like this. Being with Eden is like coming home after a long day of work. There's comfort and satisfaction and something you just can't quite put your finger on.

I lean in to ask if she wants more popcorn, but Eden shushes me because the movie is starting. I settle in beside her with a growing feeling inside my chest and a smile that refuses to fade.

• • •

Back at my place, we fall onto the bed together, and Eden wastes no time slipping her hand beneath the fabric of my shirt, placing her warm palm flat on my stomach.

A groan pours out of me, an almost desperate sound. I've been hard since halfway through the last movie. I strip out of my shirt while Eden pushes down her jeans. Soon, we're back to kissing.

She skims my chest with featherlight touches, treating me as though I'm fragile, something precious to her, and I don't know how to feel about that. But I think I like it a fuck of a lot. The terrain of this new relationship is shifting under my feet, and I'm struggling to catch up. My heart is already there, but my head? It's a mess.

The moment I decide to just go with it and stop overthinking our situation is the moment Eden climbs on top of me. I grab a condom, shove off my pants and boxers in record time, and suit up. And then she's sinking down onto me while I groan.

"Baby. *Slow*." I clench my jaw, gripping one of her hips in my hand.

"You like it?" she says softly, her voice barely above a whisper.

I groan again. "Too much."

Eden begins to move. She's incredible, and I alternate between cursing and kissing any patch of bare skin I can reach—her breasts, each wrist, the pad of her thumb that she presses into the heat of my mouth.

It's easy to lose myself in the moment—our ragged breathing, her throaty noises, the wet sound of where our bodies are joined. Sex has never been this good before.

She brings one hand between us to touch herself, and the sight of that is so erotic, so hot.

"That's it," I say to encourage her, teasing her nipples as she rides me—faster now.

I don't just want to make her feel good, I *need* it, and I love the idea that she's using my body to get herself off. Potent male satisfaction rips through me when Eden grips me tight and breathes out my name.

Her orgasm goes on and on, finally triggering my own release. I bury myself deep, and my cock jerks once as I lean up and press my face into her neck, whispering how perfect she is. She brings her arms around me, holding me close, and for maybe the first time in my life, I know what it feels like to be loved.

Eden doesn't have to say the words. Maybe

she's afraid . . . hell, I am too. I'm terrified about what will happen in the light of day.

Can she be with me? *Really* be with me without upsetting some balance in her personal and professional lives? Does she even want to?

I don't have answers to the many questions swirling inside my head. All I know is that this moment is perfect, and I don't want it to end.

23

EDEN

Three little emails. That's all that stands between me and my evening off.

Today has moved at a snail's pace, but that's probably only because I've been anticipating seeing Holt later. It'll be at a seven-year-old's party, but I'll take what I can get.

Lucian's son is celebrating his birthday today, and most of the team is going. I wish I could fast-forward to then, when I'll be sipping wine and trying to subtly flirt with Holt in front of the players. But I can't. I can only tackle the work I have in front of me.

I sigh, rubbing my temples where I can feel a headache forming. *Okay, Eden. You can do this.*

I click to open the first email, a message from

the president of one of our top sponsors. He wants to set up lunch next week.

Easy. I forward it to Aspen, asking her to fit it into my calendar. *That was painless*.

The second email, however, is not so simple. My vision blurs as I scan through multiple paragraphs of questions about media policies for next season, then reflexively reach for my phone, opting instead to hide from work in my text thread with Holt.

We've been texting on and off all day, which is doing me exactly zero favors in the focus department. Still, flirting and discussing what presents are fitting for a seven-year-old is way more exciting than media policies.

I pick up where we left our discussion on G.I. Joes, and it's not until I hear the ping of yet another email arriving in my inbox that I realize I've lost focus yet again.

Ugh. I've been chronically distracted ever since Holt and I started our . . . whatever it is that we're doing. It's not a relationship, but with our first official date under our belt, maybe it's not out of line to say that he and I are a *thing*.

However you classify our situationship, one thing is for sure—Holt Rossi is occupying more of my brain than work is lately. It's not such a bad thing considering how much I was eating, sleeping, and breathing all things Boston Titans up until recently. If I didn't step back and let myself be a human being, I probably would have imploded by now.

Still, there's a fine line between stepping back and slacking off. I still have a team to run, which sometimes means taking care of boring tasks like answering sponsor emails.

My phone buzzes in my hand, and against my better judgment, I welcome the distraction again. It's a text, but not from Holt, unfortunately.

It's from my mom, and it sounds slightly panicky. SOS! Can you swing by after work?

I gnaw on my lip, mentally budgeting my time. Two minutes ago, I told Holt I'd be at Lucian's party by six, and Mom's house is easily a thirty-minute drive out of the way. But if the situation is as urgent as her text would suggest, I might need to leave the office early. Emails can wait until tomorrow. I'm not sure if I can say the same for whatever is going on with Mom.

With my mind made up, I focus on my phone, my thumbs flying across my keyboard. Sure thing, Mom. I'll be there soon.

I power down my computer and grab my coat from its hook on the back of my door on my way out.

"I'm leaving early," I call out to anyone who might be listening, shoving my arms into my coat sleeves. "Something just came up."

Les, working diligently from his cubicle near the window, arches one bushy gray brow at me. "Is it something with Holt?"

My breath stills in my chest, and I hope my flinch isn't as visible as it feels. "What? No." I wonder why he'd assume that. Maybe I haven't been as careful as I thought.

A small smile forms on Les's lips, causing a ripple of wrinkles to appear across his kind face. "You don't have to be secretive about it, Eden. I know you a little better than that. It's clear there's something going on between you two."

Damn him for being so perceptive. And damn my brain for coming up with zero adequate responses right now. I'm just standing here, slack-jawed, blinking at him like an idiot. Thankfully, we're the only two left in the office. Aspen left an hour ago for a dentist appointment.

"Don't worry, Ms. Wynn," he says with a dismissive wave of his hand. "It's no big deal. Really. It's sweet. And you shouldn't worry about what other people think anyway."

My cheeks go warm as the tension releases from my shoulders. Les's approval is far from the be-all and end-all, but knowing someone in this office isn't repulsed by the idea of me having a *thing* with the head of security does wonders for my nerves.

"Thanks, Les," I say, my posture straightening. "But really, this isn't about Holt. I just got a weird emergency text from my mom. I'll be in early tomorrow, okay?"

He pats the top of his desk with one hand and gives me a thumbs-up with the other. "No problem. I'll hold down the fort the rest of the afternoon."

I thank him one last time before rushing out the door and straight to the parking garage.

Thirty minutes of frantic driving later, I'm turning up my mother's private drive, the sculpted hedges blurring as I pass.

It's been several months since I've been out to Brookline to visit her, and she's made more than a few changes to the landscaping in that time. Or rather, her gardener has. Each time I visit, there's some new extravagant addition—a topiary shaped like a dolphin, a marble fountain, even a miniature butterfly garden. This time, I count three new rose-bushes planted near the side gate.

I step out of my car and rush up the slate walk-way, then take the porch steps two at a time before pressing a finger against the doorbell. Penny, my mother's shih tzu, alerts the house to my arrival.

Two full minutes of high-pitched barking later, there are still no signs of my mother, and I've de-veloped a list of worst-case scenarios long enough to stretch back to my condo. I decide to take a note from Mom's playbook and let myself in from the cold.

"Hello? Mom?" My worried voice echoes through the vaulted ceilings, bouncing off the white marble pillars of the foyer.

"Sorry, sorry," her distant voice calls from up-stairs. "Be down in a second, honey. Just putting some finishing touches on my outfit."

Relief floods my system. She didn't fall or hurt herself or anything. The woman is just accessoriz-ing.

As promised, she descends the staircase mo-ments later, her sleek gray bob bouncing with every step. "Eden, honey, thank goodness you're here.

Be honest with me. Am I too old to wear this?"

She does a slow, deliberate spin, arms out to showcase her beachy outfit—a flowy cream blouse paired with turquoise capri pants. It feels awfully summery for the biting October weather we're currently experiencing.

"Not too old, but you might be too cold," I say. "It's barely fifty degrees outside."

"Not in the Bahamas." A giddy smile breaks out on her face, the stacks of silver bracelets on her wrists clinking as she claps her hands. "I just booked the cutest little bungalow for the next three months. The perfect way to get away from the cold for the holidays, don't you think?"

"Sure, sure," I say absently, swallowing the hurt building in my chest. What a way to find out I won't be spending the holidays with my mother this year. "When do you leave?"

"Tomorrow." Her expression is one of pure glee. "My flight leaves at seven a.m., which is why I needed your expert fashion advice right away."

"Right," I murmur, pulling my phone from my pocket to check the time.

Her text sounded so urgent, but playing spectator to my mother's vacation fashion show is no reason to be late for my goalie's son's birthday party tonight. When I pocket my phone again, I look up to find my mother frowning at me, her arms folded tightly across her chest.

"You can't put your work emails away for ten minutes to visit with me before I leave for three months?"

I bite back the words I so desperately want to say. *You can't give me more than twelve hours' notice that you're leaving the country for the holidays?* Instead, I heave out a sigh, finding my calm. I don't have the time or energy to pick a fight with her right now.

"I wasn't working, Mom. I was just checking the time. Is there anything besides fashion advice you needed from me?"

"Yes, actually," she says with a huff. "I was hoping you'd watch the house and take care of Penny while I'm gone."

She gestures to the ten-pound ball of fluff at my feet, and I crouch down, treating Penny to some much-deserved scratches behind her floppy little ears. She makes a happy snuffling sound and licks my palm with her tiny pink tongue. I love this little fur ball, but she's barely two years old, and much more of a handful than I have time for right now.

"I can't be driving back and forth from Boston to Brookline during the height of hockey season."

Her frown deepens. "I don't live that far from the arena, Eden."

"It's almost thirty minutes each way with traffic," I remind her, scooping Penny up and pressing to my feet. "And half the time I'm traveling with the team to away games. I have a career now, Mom. I can't just drop everything anytime you need me."

"Oh, so you care more about the Titans than your own mother." Her words are biting and overly dramatic.

"You know that's not true. You're being ridiculous." My phone buzzes twice in my pocket, and I don't have to look to know it's a notification reminding me of my plans tonight. "I have to go, Mom." Much to her disappointment, I place Penny in her arms. "I have a work thing."

"You don't have a game tonight," she says sternly.

I'm actually surprised she even knows that. "No, it's a social event with the team."

She sighs, smoothing the fluffy white hair on Penny's head. "You hear that, Pen?" she coos to her pup. "My own daughter would rather hang out at a kegger with a bunch of Neanderthals than me."

"It's not a kegger, and they're not Neanderthals," I say evenly, trying to hide the annoyance in my voice. "It's the goalie's son's seventh birthday party. As for Penny, there are multiple apps for finding reliable pet sitters."

She scoffs in disbelief. "What, so I'm just supposed to let some stranger watch my precious girl?"

I open my mouth to reply but quickly shut it, pushing back the truth. It's too painful to admit that I'm not much more than a stranger to her anyway these days. She clearly has no knowledge of what my life is like, how all-consuming my career has become. But I'm not having that conversation with her right now. Not while I have places to be and she's about to go AWOL for three whole months.

"I guess I'll have to bring Penny with me, even though she hates to fly," she mutters.

"I love you, Mom. Travel safe."

With a quick hug, I'm back out her door and into the car, feeling even more off-kilter than when I arrived. I can't press the ignition button fast enough, eager to put my mom's house in the rearview.

Soon, I'll be among friends. And it's strange to admit, but they're starting to feel more like family than my own family does.

• • •

Twenty minutes later, I pull up behind the line of cars parked outside of Lucian's house in Cambridge.

I'm a smidge late, but I'll bet the mini table-hockey game I wrapped in bright green wrapping paper will be an adequate apology. I wasn't sure if it was too on-the-nose to get the son of a goalie a hockey game, but Holt assured me it was the perfect present.

Speak of the devil, I've hardly exited my car when I spot him walking my way. He's got on a Titans shirt beneath a black bomber jacket and dark-washed jeans he fills out way too well.

Just seeing him soothes the tension left over from my visit with my mom, and I wish more than anything I could pull him in and kiss him like I did the last time we were together—hard and wild and without abandon. But there are too many people we know less than a hundred feet away, so when he reaches my side, he leans in for a quick, gentle press of his lips to my cheek, fast enough to go unnoticed by any onlookers.

"Glad you made it."

I smile at him, all the unpleasantness of my day fading away. "I never thought I'd see the day . . . Holt Rossi wearing a Titans T-shirt?"

His lips part and he shakes his head. "Only because the owner is this really cool, really hot chick I know. And I was hoping it would win her over, if you must know."

My laugh falls from my lips without warning. I love this carefree side to him.

As we walk, he tips his chin toward the box in my hands. "Let me carry that."

"I'm perfectly capable of carrying a ten-pound present," I say, clutching the box to my chest. "Plus, I don't want you taking credit for my gift."

He cracks a half smile that sends a warm, buzzy feeling reverberating through me. "Fair. Come on, I'll show you where to put it. And where to find the rosé."

"I just came from my mother's house, so yeah, wine would be greatly appreciated right now."

I follow Holt up the driveway and into Lucian's sprawling backyard, which is decorated for the season with more pumpkins than I've ever seen within the city limits. There are a few familiar faces, mostly players, gathered around picnic tables that must have been brought in for the occasion, and in the distance, the giddy squeals of first graders spill from a giant castle-shaped bounce house.

I drop my present on the table with the other brightly colored boxes, trying not to chuckle at the poorly wrapped G.I. Joe-sized box that is almost definitely Holt's.

"Let's get you a drink before I turn you loose to the team," he says, leading me to an outdoor bar on the patio.

Despite it being a seven-year-old's birthday party, there's no shortage of adult beverage options. I select a bottle of rosé, pouring myself a generous glass before locating Lucian and his wife, Camille, across the yard. They appear to be in conversation with Tate, the rookie, but when Lucian spots me, he immediately pivots away, his eyes bright with excitement.

"You made eet," he says with a grin, pulling me in for a hug that takes me totally off guard.

Maybe French-Canadians are just more affectionate than we Americans are, or maybe the team really is starting to accept me. I'm hoping it's both.

"Happy to be here." I smile, then scan the yard for any sign of a newly minted seven-year-old.

"Where's the birthday boy?"

Lucian juts a thumb toward the bounce house behind him. "Zee kids have hardly left that thing. We will have to deflate eet to get them out."

Tate snorts. "Dude, for the love of all things safety, please do not trap your son and his friends in a deflated bouncy house."

"Speaking of safety." Price St. James appears out of nowhere, slapping a hand on Holt's back. "You're not here as security, man. You're here as a friend. You don't have to be guarding the boss all night."

Heat creeps up my neck and flushes my cheeks. "Hi, Saint, nice to see you too. But I appreciate the extra layer of safety."

It's not a total lie. Being close to Holt makes me feel safe for all sorts of reasons. It's not just that he would never let me get hurt. He would also never be the one to hurt me. Unlike Alex, who has just appeared with a beer in his hands and a frown on his lips. Someone doesn't appear to be in much of a partying mood.

"Hey, Eden, did you scope out Holt's wrapping job?" Tate nods toward the gifts table, suppressing a smirk. "I thought the Titans hired a security firm, but I think this dude might be a professional

DIY-er."

Holt grunts, but before he can get a word in, he's interrupted by Saint's cackling laugh.

"DIY? What the fuck does that mean, dude?"

"Do it yourself," Tate says calmly. "What, you've never been on Pinterest before?"

The guys break out into some ridiculous argument about whether Pinterest is only for women, throwing around jokes like they're racking up points and earning plenty of laughs from everyone. Well, everyone but Alex. I haven't seen him smile once since I arrived. Not that it matters much to me. His bad mood is only my problem if it impacts his game.

"All right, is enough," Camille finally announces, clapping her hands. "Is time for presents."

As Lucian and his wife round up the kids, the rest of us take our seats at the picnic tables. There are limited spots, and I certainly don't mind fitting four people to a bench, allowing me to cozy up close to Holt by necessity.

We're close enough that he can ask me in a quiet grumble, "Is my present wrapping really that bad?"

I bite my tongue, suppressing a smile as I give

his giant thigh a quick squeeze. "Sort of. But you make up for your wrapping inadequacies in so many other more pleasurable ways . . . so I like you anyway."

It's a quiet, silly comment, but it's the first time I've admitted it out loud. I have feelings for Holt. And the more I turn the words over in my head, the more I know they're true.

24

HOLT

"You want another one, man?" Madden looks over at me with a concerned expression.

Looking down at the beer in my hands, I notice it's gone warm. While he's been rambling on about something, I've been sitting here lost in thought.

I shake my head. "Nah, I'm good."

He chuckles darkly. "You're not *good*. I don't know what you are, but whatever it is, it's the opposite of good." He grabs himself another beer and then takes a spot on the couch across from me.

When I invited him over, I was hoping to get out of my head a little bit—enjoy a casual night and a couple of beers with a friend. But so far, the mission is a failure. I can't seem to stop obsessing over this thing with Eden.

Our date the other night was transformative. For me, anyway. But I still don't know where we stand. How she really feels about me. When we're together, things are easy. Awesome. But when I step back and think about our future . . . that's where things get murky.

We're on two different playing fields, and I'm really struggling with how to rectify that, if it's even possible.

"You gonna tell me what's going on, or what?" Madden says, his tone hinting at his annoyance.

I give him a long look, trying to figure out what he's wanting me to tell him. "About?"

He rolls his eyes. "What the hell you're so hung up on."

I guess I've been more obvious than I thought, with all the shit storming through my head. "It's nothing."

He chuckles darkly. "Fine. Be an asshole."

This pulls a surly laugh out of me. "All right. I'll talk. But let's order some food."

Madden agrees and pulls out his phone. We decide on Vietnamese and place an order for delivery, and then he's back to looking at me with that same expectant expression.

"It's Eden."

His brows jump. "Yeah?"

I nod. "I told you I knew her in college. And yeah, we have a history."

He snaps his fingers. "I knew it was more than just an acquaintance thing."

Bastard. I remember that day in the gym when he pressed me for details.

"And we've started seeing each other again," I say slowly, "outside of work."

He takes another sip of his beer and waits for me to continue. "So, what's the story?"

"I honestly don't know. Things are casual, I think. I know she's serious about her career."

He nods. "Isn't her family rich? Like billion-aire rich?"

I shrug and lean back on the couch. "I don't know. I assume so. I mean, they own a freaking NHL team and all." I really don't know the extent of the Wynn's family fortune, nor do I need to. Their money doesn't concern me. "They're wealthy, yeah. Why does that matter?"

Madden meets my gaze. I mentally prepare myself for him to point out how someone like Eden Wynn would never go for a guy like me, and my grip tightens around my beer.

Instead, Madden only shrugs. "That's cool, but you're right, I guess it doesn't matter. If you've got a connection, then go for it."

He takes another leisurely swig of his drink while his words bounce around inside my head like a pinball.

Like it's so easy. Like Eden and me being together is the simplest thing in the world.

Nothing about my life has been easy, so I have zero expectations that it will start now. Still, there's something that lingers deep in my chest . . . a flicker of hope that can't be extinguished.

• • •

"Mom?" I call out as I crack open her unlocked door.

"In here," she calls from somewhere deeper inside the apartment.

I balance two bags of groceries in my arms and let myself inside. It's been a few weeks since I've seen her, and the guilt was starting to wear at me. I didn't particularly *want* to come over here today, but the desire to be a good son was eating away at me, and so here I am . . . son of the year.

When I find Mom, she's in the kitchen, coloring in a notebook.

"Hey," I say, setting the bags of groceries down on the counter. "Brought you some bananas. Soup. That bread you like. Just some basics."

"Thanks, baby." She looks up at me and smiles.

Mom looks good—there are no dark circles under her eyes, and she's curled her hair. All good signs that she's taking care of herself.

"What's that?" I ask, confused as I watch her select a yellow-colored pencil from the table.

"It's an adult coloring book." She smiles, and my eyebrows must dart up, because then she laughs. "It was a gift from my addiction counselor."

"Oh." I shove my hands in my pockets.

"Come on. I'll share." She pats the seat next to her.

With a sigh, I join her at the kitchen table. From this vantage point, I can see what the image is she's coloring. It's a farm scene—complete with hills and a barn in the background, and a bunch of baby animals in the foreground. She hands me a pencil that's somewhere between gray and brown.

"You can do that wheelbarrow." She nods to the paper.

I obey, scribbling the color onto the page while my mom watches. *This is so weird.*

"How have things been going since you got home?" I ask.

Mom smiles as she colors each daffodil on the hill a bright, sunny yellow. "Just fine. Better than fine. How about you? Still on that job with Eden?"

I know better than to believe Mom is past her addiction, but I'll take whatever good news I can get. Even if she's just trying to change the subject.

I hesitate, unsure of how much to tell her. "Uh, yeah."

Mom stops coloring to appraise me. "Uh-oh. I know that look. You've gone and fallen for her, haven't you?"

I swallow and finish coloring the wheelbarrow. "We've started spending some time together outside of work."

Mom makes a sound in her throat, then grabs a

pink pencil and gives the piglet some color.

"Say it," I say sharply. "Whatever's on your mind, just say it."

She lifts one shoulder and gives me a sympathetic look. "I worry about you, is all. Girls like Eden, they're . . . *different*, Holt. Different from you and me."

As I process her words, I realize that somewhere deep inside, I used to agree with her. I used to believe the lie that I told myself that Eden and I were just too different, that we could never work. But now I know better. And while there may be some things holding us back, it's not our economics, or the number of zeroes in her bank account versus mine.

"That's just it, Mom. Eden doesn't care that I don't have money. She doesn't bat an eyelash at my lumpy mattress, or the chip in the mug when I serve her coffee."

Mom's silent for a moment, and she pauses in her coloring to look at me.

Rising to my feet, I continue. "I'm falling for Eden, and I think she feels the same about me. If you can't accept that two people can care about each other without money having a damned thing to do with it, then I won't sit here and be lectured about it."

"I'm sorry." Mom's voice cracks. "All I ever wanted was to keep you from getting hurt like I did all those years ago. I've seen how those kind of people treat people like us."

"There's no such thing as *those people*, Mom." My tone softens. "We're all the same. We all have fears and insecurities and things about ourselves that we want to change. And we all want a shot at love."

Mom smiles sadly at me. "Then you go take your shot, baby."

25

EDEN

"**W**ould you believe me if I told you this is my first time at this beach?"

It's a rare warm day in late October—just over seventy degrees, according to my weather app—and Holt and I are walking hand in hand down the Harbor Walk, strolling from the parking lot toward whatever he has planned. He refused to tell me what's on the agenda today, and my only clues are the suspicious canvas tote slung over his shoulder, and the fact that we're walking toward the beach.

"No way," he says, arching a brow at me.

I look at him and nod. "My family used to go to the Cape several times a year. And we took plenty of tropical vacations during the winter. But this beach?" I wave my free hand toward the shoreline, dotted with clusters of happy Bostonians enjoying the weather. "I've only ever driven past it."

I'm not sure if it's the sun or embarrassment that makes my cheeks go warm, but Holt doesn't act surprised. Instead, he keeps asking questions.

"The Cape, huh? I've never been out there. How does it compare?"

"It's gorgeous," I say with a smile, my memory flooding with happy vacation moments from before my parents' divorce, back when family trips to the Cape were as frequent as bank holidays. "My mom has always been a sun-and-sand type. She usually said the beaches here in Boston were . . ."

I cut myself off, biting down on my lower lip, but Holt nods, fully understanding where I was headed.

"I get it. They have a certain reputation," he says, kicking a discarded cigarette butt in the sand to emphasize his point.

Seconds later, we reach the main entrance to the beach, but Holt doesn't halt his stride, leading us past it. When I raise a brow, he just squeezes my hand.

"I know where I'm going. Trust me."

The airy, tingling sensation in my chest spreads

through my body. I do trust him. Maybe more than I should after just a few weeks of having him back in my life.

But everything about him, about us together, sends me positive signals. Even the way he holds my hand, his fingers laced tightly with mine, but with such a gentle touch, like I'm a bird he doesn't want to fly away. Beneath his rough-and-tumble exterior, Holt Rossi is a gentle giant, and I would follow him just about anywhere.

After we've passed the busiest portion of the beach, he steers us off the Harbor Walk and through a patch of knee-high brush to a small stretch of sand that looks like it's been pulled from a postcard. Here, the crowds of families and college students are nowhere in sight. It's just the two of us, surrounded by white sand and the steady lap of waves against the shore.

I'm so enthralled by the view that I hardly notice Holt unpacking the tote bag. When I turn around, I find him sitting on a red flannel blanket, puffed up with pride as he pours wine into two travel glasses. It's a sight that makes my heart turn half a dozen backflips.

"C'mon." He pats the blanket next to him. "Let me show you what I brought."

I join him, feeling my smile widen more with each item he pulls from the tote.

A box of crackers, a plastic container holding slices of salami and cheese, and a family-size bag of my favorite honey-mustard pretzels, the kind I keep on my desk at work. A simple, romantic picnic containing all my favorite things—good wine, good snacks, and Holt.

When I reach for the bag of pretzels, though, he stops me, reaching back into the tote.

"Hold on. I haven't shown you the best part." He retrieves another plastic container from the bag, tugging off the lid to reveal bite-size bacon-wrapped goodies. "Don't worry, they're dates," he tells me with a hint of a smirk. "No shellfish this time."

A deep belly-laugh bursts from me. "Okay, that's actually hilarious," I say, popping one into my mouth. It's all the maple, bacon-covered goodness a girl could ask for without any of the emergency trips to the hospital.

We bask in the salty air, snacking and soaking in each other's company as the sun begins to sink in the sky. Today is nothing extravagant, nothing out of the ordinary, but I've never been so fully aware that this is exactly what I want. Something simple and sweet and easy. Not the fancy restaurants or dimly lit bars with overpriced cocktails other men have tried to use to impress me, as if their black AmEx cards could somehow prove their worthiness. Sitting here with Holt on a secret stretch of beach, seeing his attention to all the little details, I'm more impressed than I've ever been with a man before.

"So, tell me," I say, polishing off what's left of my wine and cozying up to Holt. "How'd you become such an expert on the beaches of Boston?"

"I used to take my little cousins here all the time," he says, sliding one big arm around my waist. He pauses for a moment, and when he speaks again, his voice is a bit strained. "After my brother got locked up and Mom got into painkillers, I became the go-to babysitter of the family. It was easier to keep them occupied here than in my aunt Lori's two-bedroom in South Boston."

His words weigh heavy on my chest. There's so much to unpack in his statement, I'm not even sure where to begin, so I trust my instincts and ask the first question that comes to mind.

"How is your mom doing, by the way?"

With my head pressed against his chest like this, I can't see his expression, but I can feel his body rise and fall beneath my cheek as he heaves a sigh. "She's doing okay. She enrolled in an outpatient program through her rehab facility to keep her on track, and they seem happy with her progress so far."

"That's good to hear. But it still has to be hard for you," I whisper.

"It's been tough forever. I'm used to it by now. Not that it ever gets easier, but you learn to adapt. Let the struggle make you stronger."

I uncurl myself from him, shifting back to meet his gaze. "Still. It's not fair, and I'm sorry you had to go through that."

"We all go through shit," he grumbles, offering a forced smile that doesn't quite meet his eyes. "I'm more concerned with how it affects you."

My brow crinkles. Of all the responses he could have given, I never would have expected that one. "What do you mean by that?"

"I've had years to get hardened to this shit. But you . . ." He shakes his head as his gaze slips away from mine. "You don't need any additional baggage."

My heart constricts at his words. He sounds so defeated, like his family life is too much for me to handle. Maybe he's forgotten that I come with my fair share of family drama too.

"We all have skeletons in the closet," I tell him, laying one hand on his. "You remember who my father is and what he did, right?"

Holt's gaze flickers back toward me, one dark brow arched. "The governor?"

"Former governor." I swallow the sour taste in my mouth that always appears when this topic arises. "I was just starting middle school when he was removed from office. As if dealing with my parents' divorce wasn't enough, having his affair with his secretary be the talk of every news outlet wasn't exactly fun. It was easy fodder for the bullies at my private school."

"Kids can be cruel."

"And adults. You know I've dealt with my fair share of grown-up bullies ever since I took on the team."

Holt's lips press firmly together as he draws in a deep breath through his nose. "I guess, in our own ways, neither of us have had it easy," he says with a sigh.

"Don't get me wrong. Your upbringing was way harder than mine. I don't want to demean that.

But just because my family has money doesn't make us any less screwed up. Believe me."

A small smile forms on his lips, his whole body relaxing as he pulls me back into his arms. "I guess we're more similar than I thought."

I nestle my head into his shoulder, breathing in his woodsy scent. "Twin flames."

We sit like this for a long moment, watching the waves roll in as he strokes my knuckles with the pad of his thumb. When he breaks the silence, it's in a voice so soft, yet so sure, it sends a wave of heat rolling through my system.

"I don't know how I got lucky enough to find you again, Eden."

Before I can respond, he lifts my face and presses his lips to mine in a warm, tender kiss that makes my whole body light up in response.

What he said is true. By some miracle, we found each other in this crazy world a second time. And I can't say for sure, but something tells me we would find each other over and over again, in this lifetime or the next.

We stay tangled up together, cuddling and kissing until the sun has sunk low in the sky. As much as I wish we could stop time in this moment, the oncoming darkness has other plans.

With the sky burning orange, we pack up our picnic, loading up the blanket and remaining snacks, and make the trek back to Holt's car. When he slides into the driver's seat, he turns toward me, his gray eyes dark with want, and asks the question I've been desperately waiting for.

"Do you want to head back to my place?"

It's the easiest, most enthusiastic *yes* I've ever given.

• • •

The drive back to Holt's apartment is short, but each minute crawls past slower than the last, each second filled with the need to be close to him, to be gathered up in his big arms again. When we finally arrive, I sink into his soft gray couch while I wait for him to put away the snacks we didn't finish.

"Can I get you anything?" he calls over his shoulder from the kitchen. "More wine? Something to eat?"

I shake my head, and moments later, he joins me on the couch, pulling me against his bulky frame, close enough that I can rest my head against his chest.

It's far from the first time we've been close like this, but something about him feels different tonight, more at ease. While he toys with my hair, running his thick fingers through my wind-tousled waves, I tune in to his heartbeat. It's a steady rhythm thrumming against my cheek, until his hand travels from my hair to my hip, then slowly begins stroking the curve of my ass. Suddenly, his pulse quickens, as does mine.

"Mmm. That's nice," I say, grinding my hips against his touch in approval.

Before long, his hand wanders to the button of my jeans, and I'm all too eager for him to help me out of them. When he spies the lacy purple thong I have on underneath, his mouth falls slack, his breath an uneven shudder.

"Fuck, honey."

His tongue sweeps over his lower lip as he drinks me in, greedy hands reaching for the scrap of lace clinging to my hips. But I have other plans. This man had the courage to share his broken past with me today, and I want to show him just how grateful I am. When I sink to my knees in front of him, a low, tortured sound rumbles deep in his throat.

"Jesus, Eden. Too good to me."

He shoves off his jeans, and a small bubble of pride forms in my chest when I see he's already half hard for me. A few gentle caresses from base to tip and he's ready, his stormy eyes pleading with mine. But he doesn't have to plead. I want him just as much as he wants me. When I slide him into my mouth, a shiver rolls from him through me, a shared moment of pure adrenaline as we connect.

"Good God, Eden."

He gathers my hair in his fist, holding my blond waves at the nape of my neck as I take an inch of him, then another, until my lips are wrapped tight around him. He shudders, and I glide my lips up to his velvety tip, then down again, working him over with my tongue all the while. Then his breath hitches and he pulls back, his ash-colored eyes flickering with something close to primal.

"So good, sweetheart. But I need all of you."

I can't argue with that.

Weaving his fingers through mine, he pulls me back onto the couch and into a deep, hungry kiss. It's not long till his mouth wanders down my neck, sucking and nipping at my collarbone and earning him a breathy moan in response. Soon, we're shedding what's left of our clothes, and I'm climbing over him, my knees pressed on either side of his thick thighs.

"Condom?" he asks.

I meet his eyes. "Do we need it? I'm on birth control, and . . ."

"Your call. I'm good if you are."

His words are strained, barely above a whisper, and I kiss his mouth and shake my head. We don't need anything else between us.

I'm wet for him already, but he dips a finger inside, testing my heat and groaning at what he finds.

"So perfect."

A shaky moan pushes past my lips as he lifts me over him, positioning me just right. I plant my palms against his firm pecs, steadying myself the best that I can. But when he guides me down onto him, sinking all the way into me, steady is the last word I'd use to describe what I'm feeling.

Good God, this man fits inside me so perfectly, like his body was made to fit into mine, two interlocking puzzle pieces finally coming together. My heart beats an uneven rhythm as I ride him, grinding my hips against his until I feel a wild heat building between my legs.

"Holt," I say on a gasp. "I'm close."

His fingers sink into the small of my back, pressing me tight against the curve of his length. "Me too, baby," he says softly. "Come for me."

I kiss him then, and with one last tilt of his hips, pleasure rolls through me in hot, wild waves. He's only moments behind me, releasing into me as he groans my name. It's sweet and glorious on his lips.

Eden. Like the most perfect prayer.

26

HOLT

Things between Eden and me are effort-less—like running downhill. It's just easy.

Over the past few weeks, we've gone on dates, hung out together at her place and at mine. Cooked. Watched movies. Talked. I've rubbed her feet while she worked on her laptop. And we've had a lot of sex . . . definitely no complaints there.

But I've noticed something else. I'm starting to feel things I have no right to.

Eden isn't my girlfriend. We aren't dating. So, why do I have a whole bunch of ideas that seem way too domestic and couple-y for what we're do-ing? Things like nights spent in bed, talking and cuddling and making love as many times as we can before my body gives out on me. Going to movies and walking on the beach.

The only time I listen to my loud, angry music anymore is when I'm working out, since I no longer need an angsty soundtrack to my life. On one hand, everything has changed, but on the other, nothing has, because we haven't actually spoken about our relationship yet.

It's something I intend to change, but I don't want to spook Eden.

I know she's only months off of a bad and very public breakup, and she's given me no indication that she's in the market for another serious relationship. She sleeps over at my place and lets me hold her. She cooks for me and texts me during the day, but that doesn't mean she's ready to be someone's girlfriend again.

"Do you want to swing by the store on the way home?" Eden asks, interrupting my thoughts. "I'd like to get the ingredients for a recipe I saw online."

Home. I love that she refers to wherever we're staying together as home.

I nod. "Sure."

We went for coffee this morning after sleeping in. Well, I got coffee. Eden got some fancy latte thing that I can't even begin to pronounce. We've spent the last few weekends like this, doing mundane things together, but I'm happy, happier than

I've ever been.

After the grocery store, she says she has library books to return, so we swing by there and are now back at her place. I unload the grocery bags while Eden locates the recipe on her phone.

"Does this look good to you?" she asks.

It's something called shakshuka. I have no idea what that means. We picked up eggs, goat cheese, tomato sauce, and a crusty loaf of bread. At the time, I didn't see how they could all be combined into one recipe together. To be honest, I still don't.

"I'll eat anything you make for me," I say, pressing a kiss to her temple.

Eden smiles and gets to work, preheating the oven and instructing me on how to crumble the goat cheese while she works on the tomato sauce. She tells me about the origin of the dish as we cook. It's North African, contains poached eggs in a spicy tomato sauce, and can be eaten for brunch or dinner.

By the time she slides the cast iron skillet into the hot oven, I'm no longer skeptical. It's starting to smell damn good in here.

While we were cooking, her phone rang a few times, but she ignored it, seeming annoyed. But when it vibrates against the counter again, I can't help but be curious. I don't want to be insecure, just want to be sure she's okay.

"Any particular reason you're ignoring your calls today?" I glance over at her.

She takes a deep breath. "It's Alex. And I have nothing to say to him."

I can't help but wonder if he calls her often. Maybe they're still in touch. Hell, maybe they're well on their way to becoming best friends again, but I know I can trust Eden, so I do, putting it out of my mind.

When the food is ready, it looks amazing, bubbling sauce with soft-cooked eggs that we eat with generous hunks of crusty bread.

I'm no longer thinking about her ex at all when we settle onto the couch together after our brunch. I pull Eden close, and she lets out a soft sigh.

"What should we do today?" she asks.

"I have an idea . . ." I press a kiss to the side of her neck, and she chuckles at my lame seduction attempt.

"Oh, do you now?"

"Yes."

I lift Eden from her spot beside me and settle her onto my lap. Her knees are on either side of my hips, causing her warm center to rest right over my quickly hardening manhood.

Her eyes sink closed and she kisses me slowly, as if she wants to savor this moment between us. I'm on the exact same page. I love being here with her like this, where we don't have to hide away or pretend we're not involved.

Eden shifts her hips, eliciting a harsh pant from my lips. I work my hands under her shirt and lift it over her head. I've just filled my hands with the soft weight of her breasts when there's a brief knock at the front door.

Her worried gaze snaps to mine. I'm about to ask her if she's expecting someone when the door suddenly opens.

"Eden? You home?" Alex's voice cuts through the pounding sound of my heart.

Eden tumbles from my lap, clutching her shirt to her chest as Alex rounds the corner and comes into view. He stops suddenly, pausing in the entryway as he takes us in—both of us flushed and standing beside the couch, Eden in her bra and frantically trying to cover herself.

"Alex?" She almost shouts the word. "What

are you doing here?"

He raises both hands, then his eyebrows jump in surprise. "Holt?"

"You'd better start talking, Braun." Frustration laces my voice, and I take a couple of steps closer to him.

"Security buzzed me in. Maybe they thought Eden and I still . . ."

His words bounce around in my head. It doesn't explain *why* he's here, but imagining a scenario in which the building security thought Alex was still on the list of people Eden would invite into her condo isn't something I want to think about too hard. I'll have that problem corrected as soon as possible, and see to it that the person responsible is terminated for negligence.

Eden ducks behind me and quickly slips on her shirt, then faces Alex. "What are you doing here?"

Alex doesn't answer. His features twist into a scowl, and his hands tighten into fists at his sides. "So, you two are hooking up now?"

His voice is rough, as though he's swallowed glass. Or maybe it's just the realization that Eden and I are an item that's a bitter pill to swallow.

"That's none of your concern," Eden says,

straightening her posture, and I place one hand on her shoulder.

Alex scoffs. "This guy? Really, Eden?"

"Be careful, Braun," I warn.

Something about the way Alex is looking at her sets my skin on fire. His eyes are filled with pain and regret, and something else I can't quite put my finger on.

He shakes his head, looking down for a moment. "I always thought there was something between you two, convinced myself I was imagining it. Because, *hello*, Eden Wynn and Holt Rossi? Nowhere on planet Earth does that make sense. But fuck, what do I know?"

His words sting like only the truth can.

"Leave, Alex," Eden says, her voice shaky.

I take another step closer. "Braun, I'm warning you. Listen to her or you're going to regret this."

"Fuck you, Rossi. Fuck both of you."

Alex practically hurls his words at us, but when he takes a step closer to Eden, that's when I lose it. I throw the first punch and have him down on the floor and restrained before he can react.

He struggles against my hold. "Let me go, asshole," he hisses, thrashing against my firm grip. "I wasn't going to touch her. I was going to hand her this."

I look down at his hand. He's holding a gold watch.

"Let him go, Holt," Eden says, sounding drained and exhausted already from this fifteen-second exchange.

I release him, and Alex is on his feet before I can barely take two steps back.

Alex extends his hand holding the watch toward Eden. "It was an anniversary gift," he says, probably for my benefit. "Take it."

Eden looks uncertain, more confused than I've seen her. Then she shakes her head. "Just keep it, Alex."

"I don't want the watch," he says, daring to take another step toward Eden. "I know it was your grandfather's. Take it."

Finally, she does. Alex blows out a long sigh and then heads for the door.

What an asshole. If it were so important for him to return that watch, he could have brought it to practice any day of the week.

The door closes, and then we're alone.

Eden sets the watch on the counter and spins to face me. Worry lines her features, and I cross the room to take her in my arms, to reassure her. But instead, she's the one checking on me, delicately taking my hand to inspect it.

It's in this moment that our story comes full circle . . . me with busted knuckles, her tending to them just like all those years ago in college. The significance of this moment isn't lost on Eden. I can see the emotion in her eyes.

"I'm fine," I say, pressing my lips to her temple. I pull her close, and she rests her head on my chest.

"It's crazy how one night can change your whole life," she murmurs.

I squeeze my eyes closed—hard—and fight off an unexpected rush of emotion. "I felt so much for you back then."

She lifts up on her toes and presses her mouth to the stubble along my jaw. When I meet her eyes, I sense there's some unspoken thought on the tip of her tongue. Instead, she just whispers, "I made the wrong choice."

We're interrupted when her phone rings again.

It better not be Alex. I heave in a deep breath

while Eden grabs the phone and checks the caller ID.

"It's Les," she says before answering it.

She puts the phone to her ear, and even I can hear the frantic tone in his voice.

"Eden?" I ask when her face falls.

She swallows hard and tells Les to give her a second. When she looks at me, it's without any of the tenderness from a moment before.

"We have a problem."

27

EDEN

Holt was at my place yesterday when Les called with the news. I ushered him out with the excuse that a work thing needed my attention.

Poor Holt, he believed me. He hadn't yet heard the news, didn't realize that everything between us had just imploded. I promised to call him later, but even as I said the words, I doubted they were true. Somewhere deep inside, I worried things were over between us—for good this time.

It's a funny thing to watch your worst nightmares come true. And by funny, I mean shocking and horrible.

When I woke up this morning to an onslaught of panicked notifications on my phone, all of which contained links to news and blog articles featuring my name, I knew that I hadn't dreamed it. And yesterday, sending Holt away had only been the tip of the iceberg. I was in for one of the worst days of my life.

All it took was one little picture. A shot of me and Holt at Lucian's son's birthday party.

Holt's back is to the camera, one arm wrapped around my waist, his hand lingering on the curve of my ass. Meanwhile, my face is clearly photographed, and it's turned up toward Holt's with a smile on my lips, looking at him like he hung the damn moon.

Out of context, it would be a pretty sweet photo. But plastered on the front page of every hockey gossip blog, it makes my stomach churn and sweat bead on my forehead.

Well. Fuck me, I guess.

The media has spun themselves into a frenzy, speculating that I'm involved with someone on the team—just like they all predicted in the beginning. No one wanted to take a young female owner seriously. After my breakup with Alex, it was suggested that I'd soon move on to another player.

My heart slams against my ribs as I scroll through the notifications on my phone, each headline worse than the last.

Titans Owner Gets Cozy with Unnamed New Beau

Wynn Scores a Goal with Titans Employee, Fans See Red

Beat It, Braun: New Titans Owner Spotted Getting Flirty with Favorite New Hire

The comments section of every article is a full-blown dumpster fire of fans typing in all caps, insisting that I'm even more of a joke than they first thought.

My heart bottoms out to my stomach, which proceeds to sink to my toes. I did the one thing that all the tabloids and gossipy hockey blogs predicted. I fell for someone involved with the team. And now all the fans see is the flirty, unfocused owner they feared I would be, and they want me out. Stat. I can almost feel my career crumbling into dust.

I throw my phone to the end of the bed, plunging my face into my pillow and releasing a scream that turns into a sob.

Fuck my whole life.

I manage to pull myself out of bed and trudge to the kitchen to switch on the coffeepot. I'm going to need a whole lot of caffeine to keep me from crawling back into bed, hiding under the covers, and never showing my face in public ever again.

I can't believe this is really happening. One of the absolute worst-case scenarios, and it's happening to me in real time.

My phone buzzes in my hand, and every nerve in my body jumps with anxiety. What now, a write-up in the freaking *New York Times*?

When it buzzes again, I work up the courage to look. It's not another text or news notification, though. It's an incoming call from Holt.

My stomach lurches, and after a few seconds of consideration, I make the difficult decision to press the IGNORE button.

Yes, this mess affects him, but it affects me more. I'm the one whose face is in the picture, and I'm the one with a career and a family reputation on the line. I need space to process this shitstorm, and as much as I'd like to cry into Holt's shoulder, I'm not sure I deserve to. I'm the one who let my guard down. I knew what the media was capable of, and yet I still went out with him in public.

A knock sounds at my door, and I groan, flopping onto my couch. "Go away."

Holt was right, it turns out. I need to have a talk with building security about who's allowed to come up to my door.

"I could go away, but then I'd have to dump out this disgusting oat-milk latte, and that's a total waste of five bucks."

I perk up a little, both at the familiar voice and the mention of an oat-milk latte. It's Gretchen, thank God. That's one shoulder I can cry on all I want without the gossip sites having much to say about it.

I force myself up from the couch and let her in, trying to ignore the pitying look in her eyes as she hands me the largest coffee cup I've ever seen in my life.

"I was in the neighborhood when I saw the news," she says, each individual word sounding like a miniature apology. "Are you doing okay?"

Part of me wants to laugh at that question. Of course I'm not doing okay. My budding relationship just got exposed on every sports blog on the internet, and pissed-off fans could come kick down my door at any second.

But I don't even have the energy to call her on that bullshit question right now. All my brain capacity is currently dedicated to reminding me that I'm a complete and utter failure.

As we settle in on the couch, I blow the steam off my latte, blinking back tears as I explain to Gretchen the backstory behind the picture.

"We were at a player's kid's birthday party," I say with a sigh. "And we were trying to keep the PDA to a minimum. But clearly, we weren't trying hard enough. I mean, I thought we'd be safe there."

Gretchen nods, her eyes narrowing, and I can practically see the question forming in her mind. "Do you know who took the picture? Maybe you could take legal action against them or something."

I shake my head. "Any of Lucian's friends or neighbors who were there could have snapped the shot and slipped it to a news outlet for a quick buck. It might have even been one of the catering staff he had there that day. Hell, for all I know, one of the news sites caught wind of a gathering of players and sent a drone."

I sink deeper into the couch cushions, half hoping they'll consume me altogether and I'll never have to face the world again. "Do you think the witness protection program would turn me away for being too lame?"

"Drink your latte," Gretchen says, gently guiding my cup toward my lips. "You always have a better perspective with some caffeine in your system."

Without a counter argument, I take a hefty sip. It's piping hot and burns my tongue a little, but at this point, it sort of feels like I deserve it.

"What you need is a killer PR team." Gretchen clucks her tongue, folding her arms over her chest. "They can smooth all of this over. They'll take the old-college-flame route, lean into the fact that Holt is an independent contractor for the team, not a direct employee . . ."

She rambles on like this for a while, spilling ideas about how to solve this mess that, come to think of it, she's partially responsible for. After all, she's the one who gave me that garbage idea about banging Holt out of my system.

But deep down, I know the truth. No matter what advice my best friend did or didn't give me, what happened between Holt and me was inevitable.

If I were more of a romantic, I might call it destiny. However you label it, it's not something I ever want to let go of. The late-night drives in his car, chasing highway signs and blaring grunge music. The sweet, quiet evenings alone on his balcony, trading bits of our pasts like rookie cards.

Every moment with him has been nothing short

of perfect, but maybe all good things have to come to an end, just like they did back at Sutton. That morning in his bed, tucked in some dim corner of a fraternity house, my fight-or-flight instinct kicked in, and I chose flight. But I never thought I'd have to face that choice with him again.

"Um, hello? E? Are you okay?"

It's not until Gretchen squeezes my hand that I realize I've been staring off into space like a sad, lost puppy who doesn't know which way is home.

"I'm fine," I lie, swallowing the tears gathering in my throat. "I think I just need a shower and a little more space to process this."

Gretchen nods, her lips firmly pursed together as she reaches for her keys. "I get it. Let me know if there's anything I can do to help, okay?"

Short of turning back the clock, or complete erasure of the world wide web, I don't think there's any saving me now.

28

EDEN

After two days of working from home, which really consisted of more panicking and doom-scrolling through comments sections than working, I finally decided to pick up the phone, but only because Les was calling.

His voice was so sweet and comforting on the other end of the line, and he didn't even mind waiting while I took a break halfway through the call to cry. Somehow, after thirty minutes of back and forth, he convinced me to come back into the office today. Whether that was a good idea or not remains to be seen. Still, I'm as shaky as a toddler trying out her first pair of skates.

I'm no stranger to facing my fears. The past several months have made me an expert in that department. Angry crowds of protesters hardly faze me anymore, and I can confidently look a full professional hockey team square in the eye and speak my mind.

But as I stand in the hallway just outside the doors of the Titans corporate office, fear doesn't even begin to describe the cold feeling that's running through my veins. Terror, maybe, mixed with a certain grade of anxiety I've never known.

But I've made it this far. No use turning back. Les's words echo in my head, keeping me from running back outside. *"Hiding won't help you."*

Of all the scary things I've faced since taking over the team, those four little words might be the most frightening of all. Maybe because I know exactly how true they are.

I can't hide forever. Which is why I'm here, shaking in my black patent-leather pumps just a few steps away from facing my new reality, a reality where everyone in the office—in the city, even—knows about me and Holt. The owner of the Titans dating the head of security. How will everyone respond? Anger? Acceptance? Ambivalence, even? I won't know until I step inside.

Over the last couple of days at home, I avoided calls from Lucian's wife, Camille, as well as Reeves, Tate, and a handful of other players, which surprised me. Even though I wasn't ready to return their calls, I doubted theirs were calls of condemnation. I imagined they were actually shows of support, which made me feel the tiniest bit better. Even if I was only imagining it.

Gretchen texted me constantly. My lack of response to her funny memes or encouraging notes didn't seem to stop her. This morning's note assured me that I was a badass with a cute butt. It made me smile, despite how miserable and alone I felt inside.

Standing here, ready to face the consequences, I take a deep breath to steady myself.

Pushing my shoulders back, I focus on taking one step at a time. *Click. Clack.* I steady my breath to the slow click of my heels against the floor as I push open the office doors. Les is the first to spot me from his desk. His unruly gray eyebrows are like two eager caterpillars leaping up his forehead.

"Eden. You're back." Surprise fills his tone until he schools his eyebrows back into place. "It's great to see you."

"Great to be here," I manage to say, reaching into my purse to finger my key ring, a reminder that my car is right outside if I need to get away fast. I run my thumb against my key fob like it's a

Buddha belly I'm rubbing for good luck. Let's face it, I'll need it.

I turn away from Les for a moment to assess the office. It's not even eight o'clock yet, so it's only the early crowd so far. The general manager's door is open a crack, a low rumble of discussion leaking out. A meeting is going on in one of our glass-walled conference rooms, and I spy Aspen scuttling around the table, clearly focusing a little too hard on not spilling the tray of coffees she's delivering.

It's business as usual here. No major fires or catastrophes as a result of my recent press. Maybe this won't be as big of a disaster as I worried it would be.

"Your grandfather would be proud of you, you know." Les speaks in a hushed tone, but even spoken quietly, those words bring a lump of emotion to my throat.

"You think so?" I ask, but I truly doubt it.

"I know so. In all the years I worked for Pete, not once did I see him back down from a challenge. Right up until the very end. He didn't go down without a fight." A small, sad smile pulls at Les's lips. "I knew you were just like him."

"Thank you," I whisper, ignoring the tingling

sensation building in my throat. "I sure hope I am."

With a smile, I excuse myself and head to my office, desperate to be out of sight before I get too emotional about my grandpa. But the universe has other plans, because as I pass by the general manager's door, it swings open. Price St. James steps out, smiling and oblivious to the fact that I was close to tears mere seconds ago.

"Hey, look who's back." A huge smile breaks out on his face. "I knew you wouldn't be out for long. In fact, I made a bet with one of the D-men about it. Thanks to you, I just won fifty bucks."

I force a smile, unsure of how to feel about the players betting on my return, but thankful that Saint was on the right side of that bet. "Thanks for your confidence in me, I guess?"

"No sweat, Eden. I mean, um, Miss Wynn." His face scrunches up as he shoves a hand through his messy brown hair. "I forget, can I call you Eden in the office? Or only when we're hanging out as friends?"

I blink up at him, temporarily rendered speechless. If you would have told me two months ago that one of the players would refer to me as a friend, I would have bet a lot more than fifty dollars that you were lying, that's for sure. "Eden is just fine."

"Well, *Eden*," he says, emphasizing my name with a wiggle of his brows. "I just wanted to say I think it's cool as fuck that you and Holt are together. He's a good dude, and you're a cool chick. Perfect match, I say."

I stiffen, all too aware that three days of ignored phone calls may have changed my status with Holt, but I'm not about to fill Saint in on that. Instead, I just murmur, "Thank you."

"Of course. But seriously, fuck the media. Those buzzards will rip you apart for anything, but it never lasts. Teddy King from the Seattle Ice Hawks had a freaking sex tape leak last year, and that dude is still playing. Plus, he's married to some hot lawyer now. Seems like everything worked out for him." Saint scoffs, shaking his head in disbelief. "A whole damn sex tape. What do you have, one picture with Holt's hand on your ass? You're fine."

My lips pull into a tight frown. "I think that only works when that person in question is well liked to begin with, and isn't a woman working against a double standard."

Saint only nods. "I can't say anything about the whole being-a-woman thing, but what I can say is the team is behind you. We like you, and we like what you're doing for the Titans. We've got your back no matter what, okay?"

His words mean more to me than I can say. I only manage a grateful smile while I try not to tear up again.

After an awkward side hug, Saint heads for the door, and I finally make it back to my office, sinking into my leather executive chair with a long sigh.

I never thought Price St. James would be the one to make me rethink this whole situation, but he made some valid points. I certainly have a lot to consider, not the least of which being where Holt and I stand.

It was wrong to ignore his calls, but I needed space to process. Now that he's no longer calling, I wonder if he's given up on me altogether.

The thought is almost too much to consider, so I turn my focus toward my email, hoping for a distraction, but it's no use. There's only one thing on my mind. Well, two, if you count both his stormy gray eyes and those big, comforting arms that, when I'm wrapped up in them, I feel like nothing could hurt me. Not a hundred hockey blogs or gossip sites. Nothing, so long as I'm with him.

That's not something I can let slip away. Not for a second time.

With my mind made up, I shove up from my desk, but before I can take even a single step, a familiar figure appears in my doorway and freezes me where I stand.

"Good morning, Eden."

The sound of Holt's low, deep voice sends an electric current from my chest to my fingertips. Just the man I was about to go looking for, and now he's here before I could even decide on the right thing to say.

I steady my gaze on the company logo stitched onto his polo, hopeful that focusing on something stationary will stop the dizzy feeling rushing to my head. It doesn't, and soon I'm collapsing back into my chair, gripping the armrests.

Holt rushes to my side, crouching down to level his face with mine. "Are you okay?"

"Fine, fine," I murmur, swallowing hard as I wave off his concern. "Just light-headed. I got up too fast or something."

Emphasis on the *or something*.

He disappears for a moment to get a glass of water from the staff kitchen, and I gladly gulp it down. It makes sense that I'd be dehydrated— I was too nervous this morning to keep anything down. But now, with Holt's big hand resting on my shoulder and his kind eyes watching closely over me, my nerves have subsided. Like always, I feel safe with him.

"How are you feeling?" he finally asks, still watching me with an expression of concern.

"Better," I say. "I should probably eat something soon, but the water helped. Thank you."

His laugh is a low, gravelly rumble in his throat. "I meant how are you feeling about everything else? And, you know." He pauses, drawing in a breath. "About us?"

His voice is thick with emotion, and when I look up at him, his gray eyes are clouded with worry, waiting for my response.

I match his question with another. "Is there still an us?"

Holt's dark brows draw together, his forehead wrinkling in genuine confusion. "What are you talking about? Of course there's still an us. That is, if you still want there to be."

"Of course I do. I just . . ." I chew my lip, searching for the right words, but nothing I say could fully encapsulate everything I'm feeling. About life, about this team, about him. With a shaky sigh, I finally manage some kind of response. "There's just so much to process."

He nods, seemingly understanding all the words I'm not saying. "I get it. I was shaken too, but I know this is a much bigger deal for you and your career. I want to respect the space you need, to let you handle it."

He gives my hand a squeeze, and I squeeze back extra hard.

"I think I'd rather handle it together."

The air between us lightens, and the tension in Holt's shoulders eases.

"I think we can do it," he says, his voice firm. "People have been accepting already. I'm sure we'll get the fans on board too."

My mouth quirks up, then quickly drops when a storm cloud of a thought rolls in. "What if they start protesting again?"

"Then you're lucky you have a damn good security team."

My heart squeezes, and the tiniest laugh bubbles past my lips. "Yeah? I heard the owner of our security company is a real tough guy."

"Not as tough as he used to be." Holt laces

his fingers with mine and guides me to my feet. "I think he developed a bit of a soft spot for the woman he's falling for."

"Falling for, huh?"

His chin dips in a firm nod as he closes what's left of the space between us. "I know what I said. I'm happier with you than I've ever been with anyone, Eden."

He brushes my hair behind my ear, his fingers trailing along the tender skin on my neck. The simplest, smallest touch, and suddenly my heart is rioting in my chest.

"Are you happy?" he asks softly.

"Yes," I whisper back. It's the easiest question I've ever answered. "I'm so, so happy with you, Holt. I don't want to have to give this up."

"Then don't. This bullshit will pass. We just need a little time." He pauses, then adds, "And maybe the help of someone who knows something about public relations."

I hold back a laugh. "That's what Gretchen said too. I guess if my best friend and my boyfriend are saying the same thing . . ." I pause, catching what I just said. "I mean, not to imply—"

Heat spreads from my chest to my cheeks, but

Holt just grins. A huge, proud smile that makes his eyes crinkle. I don't think I've ever seen him smile so wide.

"Boyfriend? I like the sound of that."

Before I can say another word, he tips my chin upward, lifting my mouth to his in a warm, delicate kiss. Soon, I'm dizzy for a whole new reason. The way this man kisses me—so sure and steady, like he's making a promise with every brush of his lips against mine. And I'm promising right back, holding tight to his shoulders like I'll never let go.

Several moments pass like this until I remember my reality, that we're making out in my office. I pull away, my eyes wide and wild as I whisper, "Shit, we shouldn't be doing this at work."

But Holt just laughs and pulls me in again. "Who cares? It's not like they don't already know."

29

HOLT

One month later

This was a terrible idea. The worst.

Eden and I moved in together a few weeks ago, and we decided to host a Thanksgiving dinner. Many players from the team are here—those without family in the area and the single guys, anyway.

Well, all except Braun.

Eden and I both bit the bullet and invited our moms because they hadn't met yet, and frankly, it was something we wanted to just get over with. And so far, it's a little awkward, but Eden and I are suffering through it together.

"Oh my God, the turkey," Eden shouts from the kitchen.

Now smelling the smoke, I turn to head in her direction. After a quick glance around the room of our mingling guests, no one seems to notice Eden's panic, so I quietly head for the kitchen to check on her. When I reach the kitchen, thick black smoke billows from the oven door before Eden snaps it shut.

When she turns to face me, I can see the frustration and disappointment written all over her face. Her lower lip trembles, and I capture her chin in my hands, touching my thumb to her mouth.

"It's totally ruined," she says with a sigh.

"Hey. Shake it off, sweetheart."

"But—"

I silence her with a kiss. "Nothing is ruined. I have a plan." I give her a wink. "Just breathe."

She draws a deep breath through her nose and then lets out a little cough, because it really is smoky in here. I unlock and then push open the kitchen window, hoping some air circulation will help.

"What's your plan? Order pizza? Nothing's open, Holt. We're screwed!" She throws her hands up dramatically.

Eden looks as though she could cry, and I know

it's not really about the turkey. I know she wanted today to be perfect. I know she's felt the pressure of having such big shoes to fill ever since her grandfather died. I know she hates disappointing people. And I know she *really* hates looking like a fool in front of her mother.

Which is why I wasn't going to leave anything to chance today . . . or let anything go wrong. She has to be reminded that—as I've told her on more than one occasion—I'll always protect her.

"Holt?" she says, her tone pleading.

I press a quick kiss to her pouting mouth. "Okay, so I saw this flyer . . . for that fancy grocery store down the block you like?"

"Fleishman's?" Her eyebrows push together.

I nod. "That place, yeah. They were advertising whole roasted turkeys on Thanksgiving. I ordered one . . . just in case."

"Okay, this might be worse than me burning the turkey. You *knowing* I was going to fail is so much worse."

Frowning, I shake my head. "That's *not* what this is."

Her eyes widen and lock onto mine. "Then how can you possibly explain this?" She plants her hands on her hips.

I give her shoulders a squeeze. "I know how much hockey players eat. I was only thinking . . . in case we needed more food. You know, like the pizza that you had to order the last time you had the guys over?"

"Oh." She softens, her mouth lifting in a smile. "Oh. Yes. That was . . . *thank you*. That was probably a good idea."

I grin back at her. It's the truth.

"But how do we—"

I silence her with another quick kiss, because it's just really damn satisfying being her knight in shining armor right now. "Aspen is picking it up on her way over. She'll be here any minute. And everything's fully cooked, so we'll just have to plate it."

"Everything?" Her eyebrows lift again.

I shift my weight. "So, I actually got *two* turkeys. Three more pumpkin pies, and a side of mashed potatoes."

Her eyes widen. "Is that all?"

I shrug, giving her a sheepish look. "And a ham, extra gravy, and two dozen garlic rolls."

She laughs. "Oh my God, you're insane but I love you."

"I love you too."

Eden looks at her kitchen island, gesturing to the food set out there. "But I baked six apple pies and two pumpkin—"

"I know, sweetheart. Again, it's just in case. Hockey players eat like six thousand calories a day during the season." She should know this. After all, she's the one who once told me that factoid.

Eden rolls her eyes and crosses the kitchen to turn off the oven. I take a moment to check out her ass. It's a wonderful sight, what can I say?

When Aspen arrives a few minutes later, I distract Eden's mom with some riveting questions about her shih tzu's diet—more than I ever wanted to know—while Eden and Aspen shuffle quietly into the kitchen to remove all the food from the plastic and tin containers and onto serving platters.

A few minutes later, we're all seated at two long tables that have been set up in the living room and decorated by Eden herself.

Last week, she called me incredibly excited on her way home from a craft store, where she'd found fake pine branches, autumn leaves, miniature pumpkins, pine cones, and a whole bunch of white votive candles that she somehow turned into a professional-looking centerpiece for each table. It's very impressive.

I'm next to Eden, and our moms are across the table from us, still chatting away. This time, the topic is the best place to get a manicure. The guys are scattered around the two tables—it's no shocker that Alex isn't here. We're not on bad terms with him, but let's just say things are still awkward.

Wild takes the seat next to Eden's, and Les and Aspen are across from him. Saint pulls out the chair beside mine, and once everyone has found a place, Eden stands and clasps her hands in front of her.

"You guys," she says, laughing unexpectedly. "Who knew we'd be *here* together?"

A few of the guys laugh.

I know she doesn't mean here, *physically*, eating Thanksgiving dinner together, but *here* in these deep relationships, these friendships and team camaraderie that has formed so unexpectedly.

She's right. Everyone has grown close this season, and it's all because of her. It's obvious the team shares a deep bond that's allowed them to rise to the top of their division.

And as for me? Eden is my whole world, and that's the last thing I expected when I walked in her office that day after accepting a new assignment. But let's just say I have a lot to be thankful for this year.

"I'm truly blessed to call this team my own, and I'm thankful you all chose to be here, spending the day with me. Cheers, everyone!" Eden raises her water glass in a toast.

"Cheers!" and "Happy Thanksgiving" is echoed around the room.

And then a couple of the players stand. At first, it's just Saint and Reeves, followed by Lucian, Miles, and Tate. And then everyone is standing, all nine of the hockey players here today. And they're all looking at Eden.

I expected them to dig into their food the second her toast was done, but instead, everyone is unnervingly silent, and I'm not sure what's happening.

Saint runs one hand over the back of his neck, looking a little sheepish. "We, uh . . . the guys and I came up with something we wanted to say." He nods to Reeves.

Reeves begins with a confident smile. "E is for the encouragement you've provided since day one."

"D is your determination. It's second to none," Lucian says in a serious tone, giving Eden a meaningful look.

I find her hand under the table and squeeze it. Her eyes are wide, and there's a slight smile on her mouth, but she also looks surprised, like this is the last thing she was expecting.

"E is for the excellence you demand in everything you do," sings Tate.

"And N is for your no-bullshit attitude, which we appreciate too," Miles says, getting a few laughs from around the table.

"There's no one else we'd want at the helm, and to this I say kung-fu," Saint finishes.

"Kung fu?" Wild asks.

"I needed something to rhyme with *too*," Saint whispers, which gets a few chuckles.

"To Eden!" everyone shouts at once.

I raise my glass in a toast to her and then lean over to steal a kiss. "I think your hockey team just wrote you a poem."

Tears glisten in Eden's eyes when she gazes at me and nods. "I think so too."

Even Eden's mom looks stunned by their thoughtful display.

"I love you all, but you're jerks for ruining my mascara." Eden laughs, wiping her eyes with her cloth napkin.

The guys chuckle, some calling out, "We love you too!"

"Now, eat," she orders them with another shaky laugh.

And they do. Everyone digs in with gusto. I can barely keep up with carving the turkeys, and the ham is gone before I can even blink. In addition to playing a rather rousing game of hockey, these guys have an impressive talent for making food disappear.

Camille and Lucian ask about a few of the dishes they're not familiar with. The sweet potato casserole with marshmallows seems to amuse them, though Lucian dishes out a second helping for himself, grinning as he eats. "Is good."

The pies are sliced and coffee is served, and everything is delicious. By some miracle, we have plenty of pie.

As I glance around the room—seeing Eden at the center of an animated conversation about save percentages and the western conference standings, and which is better, pumpkin or apple pie—I can't help but smile.

I'm happy for her. She once admitted to me she didn't have many friends, during one of those late-night, post-sex conversations—you know, the kind where you can really let your guard down? Well, she opened up. Her voice was soft, almost as though she was letting me in on a dark secret.

And maybe she was, because I was sure as hell shocked to hear she felt that way. Everyone who meets Eden loves her, and most probably think she's out of their league. I couldn't figure out why she'd struggle to make friends, because she's friendly, open, bright, and articulate.

But seeing her here now, surrounded by a loud team of hockey players and her staff, it's obvious she's found her tribe. This crew would do just about anything for her.

Maybe she was just waiting for her people, and now she's found them. We would be here for her through thick or thin, through exciting wins or bitter losses. We'd see her through her bullies and critics, and definitely be there to celebrate with her in the good times—like this one.

Because for as much as I complained about today, there's a lot to be thankful for. Eden's mother came back to the US for the holidays, which I think secretly pleased Eden. And by some miracle, my mom is actually getting along with her mom.

Eden laughs at something Saint has said, and then she looks at me, flashing me the most brilliant smile that sends a jolt straight through my chest. It's then that I know I'm so damn lucky to be the guy by her side. It's a place I'll gladly stay for all of eternity, next to her, letting her take the spotlight and shine like the star she is.

Because it doesn't get much better than this. A beautiful woman who loves me, plenty of pie, a totally burned turkey, and a bunch of rowdy hockey players reciting horrible poetry.

EPILOGUE

EDEN

The only thing better than Thanksgiving dinner is the long, turkey-induced, night's sleep afterward.

When I blink awake in the morning, nine full hours of shut-eye later, I feel as though I'm waking up from a coma, more rested than I've felt since the hockey season began. I guess that's what a full belly, a night with friends, and the perfect bedmate does for you.

When I sit up to check the time, the big burly man next to me grumbles, pulling me closer to him like I'm his favorite teddy bear.

"Morning," I murmur, snuggling closer into Holt's broad chest. His body is warm and solid against mine, one arm draped protectively over me.

"Mmm, nope." His voice is hoarse with sleep, and he buries his face in my hair. "I reject that. It's still nighttime."

"I think the sun says otherwise." I chuckle, allowing just enough space between us for me to roll over and face him.

The tips of our noses brush against each other, which brings a slight sleepy smile to his lips, even though his eyes remain closed. I don't think I've ever seen him this peaceful, this content.

"Rise and shine, baby," I say, squeezing his hip. "We need to get on the road soon."

It's rare that we both have a day off, so we decided to make the most of our long holiday weekend and book a getaway to the Cape. We picked out the cutest little family-owned inn for our stay, and this afternoon, I'm surprising him with a private whale-watching excursion out of Provincetown.

In just a few hours, we'll be bundled up in the back of our own private charter boat, watching the waves through sets of binoculars. That is, so long as I can get Holt up and moving in time. Luckily, I know how to wake him up in a hurry.

"C'mon, sleepyhead," I murmur, guiding my hand along the front of his boxer briefs.

His body jerks in response, and he instantly stiffens beneath my touch, just as I hoped.

"Mmm, yeah?" His gray eyes flutter open, already dark with need as he touches his lips softly to mine.

One hand floats up to my jaw, and when he kisses me again, we're suddenly both wide awake. He plants a trail of lazy, open-mouthed kisses along my neck and down my collarbone, while I fist my hand around his shaft through the cotton of his boxer briefs. He sucks in a breath through his teeth, pushing his hips against my rhythm.

And then, in a moment of pure bad timing, my phone buzzes on the nightstand. I try to ignore it, keeping my grip on his length, but then it buzzes again. I'm getting a call.

With a sigh of defeat, I slip out of Holt's arms, reaching for my phone. It's Coach Wilder.

"I have to take this." I scramble out of bed and lunge for my robe, making myself feel decent enough for a work call, then wedge the phone between my ear and shoulder. "Hello?"

"Eden." Wild sighs, sounding relieved. "Thank God you picked up. I didn't wake you up, did I?"

"No, you didn't," I grumble, because technically, that's the truth, although his call is certainly an unwanted interruption.

"Good. Any chance you've heard from Braun recently?"

My brows scrunch together at the mention of my ex, and Holt definitely notices. He sits up in bed, arching one thick brow at me. I mouth the words *it's fine* before slipping out to the kitchen.

Something about discussing an ex in my bedroom, even in a professional capacity, feels wrong, especially when my boyfriend is half-naked and probably still hard between my sheets.

"I haven't spoken to him in weeks," I say to Coach once I'm safely in the kitchen, leaning up against the island and chewing on a hangnail. "Other than a word or two at practices. Why do you ask?"

A low, frustrated noise comes over the line. "I really hate to involve you in this, Eden, but we might have a bit of a problem."

"What kind of a problem?"

"An Alex-is-missing kind of a problem. He wasn't at practice on Wednesday, and he skipped morning skate today. It's not like him."

My stomach squeezes into a tight knot.

Coach is right. That isn't like Alex. In all the years I've known him, he's never let anything stand between him and his hockey career. If he's skipping practice, he must be either sick as a dog or in a ditch somewhere. And the man may have broken my heart, but I don't wish either of those things upon him. Especially not the second one.

I promise Coach that I'll do what I can to help the situation, although I'm not entirely sure what that entails, then end the call with a huff, leaning heavily against the kitchen counter.

Holt and I need to be on the road in an hour if we're going to stick to our plans. How much can I get done in an hour? I suppose we could go to Alex's apartment and check on him before we leave town, but that feels all kinds of awkward.

I tap on my phone screen, pulling up my contacts. If ever there was a time to delegate, it's now.

Moments later, I'm on the phone with Aspen, interrupting what's supposed to be her day off too. "I'm so sorry to do this to you, but will you go check on Alex? He's not showing up to practice, and Coach is worried."

"Sure thing."

When Aspen agrees cheerily, I make a mental note to double the holiday bonus we budgeted to give her.

Just as we're finishing up our call, two big, warm arms encircle my waist, and I instantly feel at ease.

"Everything okay?" Holt asks once I've hung up, leaning over to press a kiss onto my cheekbone.

"I'm not sure. Coach is worried about Alex. He's been missing from some practices lately."

"Sounds serious," Holt replies with a grunt, which is really the most sympathy I could ask from him on topics pertaining to Alex. He knows that my involvement with my ex starts and ends with his work on the ice, but when he's not showing up to do that work, we have a problem.

"It might be serious," I say, grabbing Holt's big hands and pulling his arms tighter around me. "Or he might just be throwing some kind of temper tantrum. Either way, I've got Aspen taking care of it. You and I have other plans this weekend."

"We sure do, baby. I'm proud of you." He hums against my neck, his curious hands wandering down my hips. "Now, where were we earlier this morning?"

Before I can respond, I feel my feet lift up from the tile, and soon I'm slung over Holt's shoulder, squealing and kicking my feet as he carries me back to bed.

"We have to leave soon," I say with a laugh as my head hits the pillow, but Holt just shakes his head, smiling and pulling the tie on my robe loose like he's unwrapping an early Christmas present.

"We've got all sorts of time," he says to assure me.

And in my heart, I know he's right. We have all the time in the world. Because a man like Holt only comes around once in a lifetime. Twice, if you're lucky like me.

And now that I've found him, I'm never letting him go.

• • •

Ready for more? Up next in this series is Alex and Aspen's story, and believe me, you do *not* want to miss this!

What to Read Next

the RIVAL

Dump my cheating ex? *Check.*

Land an amazing job with Boston's professional hockey franchise? *Check.*

Fall stupidly in love with hockey's favorite bad boy? *Ugh.*

After wasting years of my life with the wrong person, I told myself all I wanted was a little no-strings fun. Enter Alex Braun—the wealthy, handsome, and notorious playboy who is equal parts charming, and dangerous as hell to my wounded heart.

After enduring a very public breakup of his own, the sexy player doesn't want to be anyone's forever. Too bad he barreled his way into my heart, instead of just my bed.

But this professional athlete knows a thing or two about competing, and he won't let go so easily.

Warning: This romance contains one grumpy, emotionally damaged, but gorgeous-as-hell hockey player, and a whip-smart, hardworking heroine who has never quite fit in. It should only be read by those who like their men brawny and their romances red-hot!

Get Two Free Books

Sign up for my newsletter and I'll automatically send you two free books.

www.kendallryanbooks.com/newsletter

Follow Kendall

Website

www.kendallryanbooks.com

Facebook

www.facebook.com/kendallryanbooks

Twitter

www.twitter.com/kendallryan1

Instagram

www.instagram.com/kendallryan1

Newsletter

www.kendallryanbooks.com/newsletter/

Other Books by Kendall Ryan

Unravel Me

Filthy Beautiful Lies Series

The Room Mate

The Play Mate

The House Mate

Screwed

The Fix Up

Dirty Little Secret

xo, Zach

Baby Daddy

Tempting Little Tease

Bro Code

Love Machine

Flirting with Forever

Dear Jane

Only for Tonight

Boyfriend for Hire

The Two-Week Arrangement

Seven Nights of Sin

Playing for Keeps

All the Way

Trying to Score

Crossing the Line

The Bedroom Experiment

Down and Dirty

Crossing the Line

Wild for You

Taking His Shot

How to Date a Younger Man

Penthouse Prince

The Boyfriend Effect

My Brother's Roommate

The Stud Next Door

The Rebel

For a complete list of Kendall's books, visit:
www.kendallryanbooks.com/all-books/

CPSIA information can be obtained
at www.ICGtesting.com
Printed in the USA
LVHW111648011021
699240LV00007BA/574